The Pace-Lap Blues and Other Tales from the Seventies

—m—

Short Fiction by Chris Dungey

ISBN: 1497541786
ISBN 13: 9781497541788
Library of Congress Control Number: 2014906484
CreateSpace Independent Publishing Platform
North Charleston, South Carolina

This book is dedicated, with love, to my wife and best proofreader, Sharon.

Table of Contents

The author would like to thank the publications, both print and online, in which some of these stories first appeared: "Pace-Lap Blues," *CACTI;* "Prep Work," *riverbabble;* "Pot-Luck Wedding Reception Blues," *Subterranean Quarterly;*" "A Hot Hand," and "Superficial," *Coup d'Etat;* "Water Test," *Squalorly;* "Muscle," *Midwest Coast Review*; "Double Fault," *Storm Cellar;*" "Photo Finish," *Winewood Journal.*

Cover photo licensed from the work of Pete Lyons. Other beautiful racing photos from the Can-Am era can be viewed and purchased from Petelyons.com.

The Pace Lap Blues

Driving across the Blue Water Bridge into Canada could be a significant political act in those days. But we weren't draft dodgers, and I wasn't carrying anyone into exile. My own student deferment had evolved seamlessly into a four-F when I dropped out of college. I clung to a summer job at Generous Motors despite low seniority then took my Selective Service physical in Detroit. The doctors listened to my lungs, read the letter from my allergist, and waved me through.

The inspiration for the road trip was my birthday and my girlfriend cheating on me one week before. She pleaded boredom because I was stuck on the nightshift. Happy Birthday to *me*! She said that the *Annie Green Springs* wine they passed around the bonfire out at the gravel pit had clouded her inhibitions. Well, she was still in high school, not too experienced at drinking, and had few inhibitions to begin with. I forgave her because she asked me to, though I was still pretty pissed off at Steve Sherman who I had thought was a pal. Steve wasn't invited along as we headed east toward Port Huron. It was about 11pm on a muggy Saturday evening in June. At midnight, I would attain my so-called *majority*. Three of my younger friends (older friends were either in the army or pushing ahead with college), who hadn't yet balled Gwen (that I *knew* of) were anxious to be along with me when the magic hour struck. After a quick circuit of their homes to gather sleeping bags, we hit the road.

"What kinda race are we going to, Hector?" Andy Ritten asked from the back seat. I didn't know Andy very well. He happened to be standing with the others when I rolled up on Terry Wickersham with my plan. They were all hanging out uptown in Celeryville, smoking cigarettes at the usual park bench, debating whether to head for the teen dance at the Legion Hall.

"It's called the Can-Am Challenge. They run prototype sports cars built just for racing. Unlimited engine size and world class drivers."

I had always been interested in motor sports. This resulted only in a few trips to local dirt ovals to watch stock cars. I learned about the Can-Am Series from a racing magazine I bought to read during down-time at work. There was a long article about Bruce McLaren, the car builder and driver who had dominated the series. McLaren had been killed two weeks before during testing. The race at Mosport would be the first event without him driving one of the sleek, orange machines which bore his name.

"We used to go to the track down at Mt. Clemens before my dad moved out," Andy said. "That was stock cars."

"But there'll be a lotta chicks?" Dick Lester leaned forward to wheeze his smoke into the front. I could see his pinched face in the rearview; a permanent, cynical scowl that showed more defeat than menace.

"Dick. Crack a window, will ya?" Terry, riding shotgun, glared into the back seat.

"How much is it to get in?" Ritten asked. "I only brought twenty bucks."

"I don't know. It's a road course so we'll just sit on a hillside or find a spot along the fence. You'll get a break for your American money."

"Wick, you still *owe* me five for helpin' at your old man's store," Lester complained.

"And I'm holding onto it for your share of the beer and all the smokes you're gonna mooch."

"Yeah, and when does *that* finally happen?"

"We've gotta hang around Port Huron until midnight, then I'm legal," I explained again. "They don't sell alcohol in Canada on Sunday. We'll have to go easy until we get to the track."

"Right. That's a bummer though, huh?"

Wickersham raised up again and turned. "Look. We can let your bony ass out right now, if you're gonna whine all weekend. You'll be getting hammered soon enough."

"I'm cool. I'm cool. Geez. Don't get your tit in a wringer."

Wickersham turned back to fiddle with the radio. My economy model Ford Maverick didn't have FM and we'd already lost WTAC from Flint in the night static. He found CKLW out of Windsor. It came in strong though we'd all begun to scoff at Top 40 radio.

"I've never met *this* grandma," he said. "She still tends bar? That's cool."

My plan was to stop downtown at *Rosedale Inn* near the hockey arena. My Gramma Mills might even front us a case for my birthday present. "In a way," I said. "My mom wants her to retire, but I guess it keeps her involved. Plus she only gets some kind of minimum Social Security."

"You do what ya gotta do, right?"

Then I heard grandparent stories until we merged onto the new freeway for the last eight miles into Port Huron. I turned north on Military Avenue. I had hitchhiked the route many times. Now I missed, for the briefest moment, my student life at Port Huron College. I had put my education on hold for a blue collar job in an auto plant, and the new car and steady girlfriend that went with it. But if contract talks that fall achieved our goals, I'd be able to resume my studies at company expense. Still, there were memories that fringe benefits couldn't replace.

"I've been *here* before," Andy Ritten said. "I saw *Paul Revere and the Raiders* at the arena."

"Ever been to a hockey game?" Dick drawled.

"The *Flags*? Many times," I said.

"Hey, Fritch. Remember when we drove to Harbor Beach last winter so you could watch Gwen cheerleading?" Wickersham was grinning slyly at the last stoplight before McMorran Arena.

"Yeah? What about it?"

"You made us listen to the *Red Wings* all the way home? Didn't we nearly kick Dick's ass out up around Bad Axe somewhere?"

I pulled ahead at the green light and put on my left turn blinker. "I believe there *were* some harsh words."

"Up yer's, Wick," Lester muttered. "I like sports just fine. What'd *you* ever play? About one year of Little League?"

"Band kid and proud *of* it," Terry laughed. "You going back to adult high school this year?"

I turned down the first side-street north of the arena. It was twenty minutes 'til midnight. Twenty minutes before official adulthood. Though there seemed to be lots of traffic moving in the sultry evening, there weren't more than four cars parked by *Rosedale Inn*. The place relied mostly on hockey games and other events next door. I suppose they did a decent lunch trade with business people and shoppers downtown.

I parallel parked and told the guys, "Behave yourselves. Don't be fighting over the damn radio. I won't be long." I walked under the humming neon above the tavern entrance. An air conditioner protruded from a glass-block window, its rusty condensation dripped to the sidewalk. Inside, the cold smacked my sweaty face.

Gramma Mills was sitting at the end of the bar, having a cigarette. She was back-lighted by the kitchenette, its café doors hooked open. The rest of the place was illuminated entirely by beer advertisements, exit signs, and the silent juke box.

All heads turned briefly as I entered: One couple at a table finishing hamburgers and drafts; two regulars, well spread out at the bar, nursing mixed drinks and cigarettes. A television above the far end waved the Stars and Stripes to end its day. Superimposed fighter planes swept above it. Someone was probably singing if the volume had been turned up.

"Well, what in the…? I'll *be*," Granmma Mills declared as I approached out of the murk. "Sonny!"

She had begun, a couple years ago, to refer to me with the moniker she'd hung on her son-in-law, my dad. I hoped it was a tribute to my maturity and not just her mind slipping. She climbed down from the stool and we hugged. She wore simple short-order whites instead of her black waitress uniform.

"Can I get my first legal drink in here? I hoped you'd be behind the bar."

"Oh no, that's a *young* fella's game. I don't keep up with all the news and sports enough to carry on conversation. They only need me to cook. I can *fry* you something."

It was then that I noticed she was wearing a hairnet. "Well, *I'm* not putting you back over that grill."

"Are ya sure? We've still got the best burgers in downtown. Dayshift does, anyway. The paper took a poll."

"Nah, Gramma. Let me take a rain-check. I'm headed over the bridge with some friends to a car race near Toronto. For my birthday."

"That's right! I just now got it, what you meant about your legal drink. I'll *be*. You know, I think I put your card in the mail yesterday. You shoulda got it."

I kept my arm over her shoulder. She was growing smaller each time I saw her. I'm not that tall, myself, but the process had accelerated now that I wasn't in town to see her more. Her white hair was a puff of gauze with the kitchen light behind her. "I haven't been out to the folks' in a few days."

"That's *right*! Your own apartment, too, I heard. I'll *be*. Well, you're lucky you got here. I think Roy wants t' close early. I woulda *missed* you. Hey, Roy," she called into the back. "C'mon out an' tend some bar!"

"Christ, Hanna! I'm getting ready to balance out!"

"Nah, c'mon out and meet somebody! Take this fella's money!"

The owner, nearly as wide as he was tall, waddled out of an office at the back of the kitchen. He took up most of the kitchen entrance.

"This here's my grandson, Hector," Gramma told him. "He's just turned twenty-one a few minutes ago."

"Good to know ya," Roy said, extending a massive hand. "Show me some ID an' I'll pour you a free one. But it'll be just one 'cause I'm starting my books."

I took my hand off Gramma's shoulder. "Actually," I hesitated. I didn't really need a free one but didn't want to sound ungrateful. I needed road beers, in quantity, and to be back *on* the road. "I'd love to hang out, but we're running behind already. I'm taking some friends to a car race in Canada. The *Brewer's Retail* isn't open on Sundays, as you probably know."

"And you're gonna want me to put the tape back in the till."

"If it wouldn't be *too* much trouble. We could use a couple of cases."

"Whoa up, son! You want me to sell that much alcohol all at once to an amateur?" Roy shook his head in doubt. "They'll probably confiscate it at Customs, anyway. You sure you wanta throw away your good money?"

"See, that's the thing. We aren't even drinking until we get to the track." I sort of resented being called an amateur drinker after enduring two years at Port Huron College. I kept my voice low and steady, but my face probably looked like that of a kid begging for the keys to the family car.

"We can put that in the drawer Monday morning, Roy." Gramma Mills had fired up another cigarette.

"Yeah, yeah, Hanna. I'm way ahead of you. Just lemme think," he sighed. "Might help save a slow night if I don't land in court at some point."

"Sure," I chimed in. "And you can round up the bill off the chip rack; some chips and pretzels."

Roy pinched the bridge of his nose. "Well, OK. Let's see this famous ID. Hanna, find a large take-out bag for the groceries."

I ended up dropping thirty bucks. Roy took the bills straight into the office. Gramma Mills shook open a grocery bag and began counting in the salty snacks. From under the bar she plucked a tall jar of beer nuts. She winked and shoved it to the bottom. Then she carried the sack into the kitchen. After Roy lugged two cases of *Pabst Blue Ribbon* in cans from the storeroom, she had the snacks ready to go. I smelled hamburger buried in there somewhere--probably take-outs that hadn't been claimed. Probably her evening meal and Sunday dinner, too.

"They're warm. Sorry. We don't have the cooler space for cases," Roy said. "And you'll have to lug them out yourself. I don't wanta see how old your *friends* are."

I hugged my Gramma again. "I'm gonna get over here for lunch," I claimed. "I miss that. I loved those home-cooked meals when I was at school."

"This is about all the cookin' I *do* any more. I'm supposed to come out t' Sis's next weekend, though," she said. "So they can keep better eye on me, I suspect. You come on by. You shouldn't be at odds with your folks all the time."

"I'm mostly not," I assured her. Matters of hair length, scholastic sloth, and general dissipation had smoothed out since I moved into my own place. I kissed Gramma on the cheek. When she started to follow with the grocery bag, I told her I'd come back for it. "I've held you up long enough. You'd be cleaned up and on your way home by now."

I carried the beer out. I told Dick and Andy to lift their feet. We put a case on each side of the floor in the backseat. When I went back in for the chips, I heard Gramma scraping the grill. The café doors were shut.

Terry put the rations between his feet. I hung a u-turn then back toward Military. I drove easy, past where the highway forked into Pine Grove Avenue. The apartment I shared last year with two other students was in that block; the Sinclair gas station where we went for pop and snacks. It was closed. I wanted to gas up before crossing, but in another block we were onto the bridge access. I would just have to figure out liters instead of gallons on the other side.

"Don't you wanta bury those beers in the trunk?" Terry asked.

"I'm not sure we even have to hide them," I said. "But here's what I'm thinking. We'll leave them hidden in plain sight. They might shine a light back there, but if they're *really* interested they'll have us park it for a trunk inspection."

"You've been through this hassle before?"

I had, in fact, crossed many times with student friends, several of whom were Canadians. We seldom had a problem. "Only once. We went to a concert at Point Edward. A couple of longhaired dudes made them curious. It was an American band with a big following. Lots of kids going over must have irritated them. You guys might wanta tidy up a bit."

I threw a couple of quarters into the toll basket and headed up the incline. It was dark below. I saw one ore freighter, lit up like a used-car lot, plowing in off Lake Huron. I think the guys missed the scenery, frantically combing hair out of their eyes.

"Could you put the dome light on?" Andy Ritten leaned over the seat to use the mirror. I concentrated on staying safely on the inside lane. Bridges made me nervous. Lester, too, appeared in the rearview frame. When he tried to tuck in his t-shirt, a cigarette pack fell from his sleeve, and he dove after it. As we coasted down the other side toward Canadian Customs, I wondered what all the activity must look like to the vehicle behind us. Even Terry flailed away at his mountain-man mane with a pocket brush.

I eased ahead. "Make it look casual back there. Don't wrap those cases up completely."

"I put my jacket over one," Dick said.

"Just partially, OK? Don't draw attention to it. What else have we got?"

"A couple of Coke bottles," Andy said. "Dick's *Three Musketeers* wrapper. Some kinda lug wrench and an umbrella under your seat."

"Right. Pull that junk out and lay in on your case. But casual."

I don't know why Customs didn't point us directly over to the office. Maybe the guy was tired after a long evening of Yanks coming to play bingo at Point Edward Casino. Maybe we just looked like welcome greenbacks. I, personally, still looked like a good citizen. I hadn't been out of my parent's house very long. And it *was* a new car. Maybe he was a race fan. He knew where Mosport was and told me "You've got quite a ride, yet." He aimed a flashlight into the backseat only to compare faces with the IDs.

"Just pop the trunk for a second. Are you bringing agricultural or tobacco products in for other than personal use?"

"No, sir." I turned off the ignition and hopped out. He poked curiously at our sleeping bags, Dick's ratty quilt, and the industrial size transistor radio someone had brought along.

"You fellas have a safe trip, ay?" He handed me all four driver's licenses, including Andy's which clearly showed him to be sixteen. It occurred to me then that the usual Canadian arrogance toward American beer might be working in our favor. Who would bother bringing in our diluted piss when *Molson* and *LaBatts* were available? And who would prefer to drink it?

The sigh of relief was collective. "I think I heard Dick's sphincter open back up," Terry laughed. Dick laughed, too, as I eased away from Customs. The currency exchange booth was closed so it looked like we'd be doing math all weekend. The first test would be to fill the tank. I turned right, off the 402 freeway onto the business route where we could find gas. An Esso station with adjoining convenience store was open. Everyone got out to stretch. I took a collection for gas and ice. The guys gave me a dollar each; more than I sometimes got out of them for cruising. We all used the bathroom. I told the old attendant to top it off. The guy was clearly an immigrant himself, wearing some kind of Sikh turban.

You couldn't buy alcohol, but Terry and Dick were amazed by the variety of rolling papers and other paraphernalia.

"Please tell me you're not holding," I thought to ask, too late.

"Not me," Terry said. "I'd be asleep by now."

"I've got a few *Christmas Trees*," Dick said, referring to the widely used truck-driver amphetamine. "They're in a baggy in my shorts."

"What if they'd strip searched you?"

Dick shrugged.

"For future reference," I began. "Oh, never mind. I wouldn't *wanta* know."

"Damn, I hope I'm never tired enough to ask you for one of those," Terry told Dick. He picked out a flat box of *Rothman's* navy cut smokes.

"Get a couple of large coffees, will ya?" I took a small, Styrofoam cooler with rope handles from a stack. When I paid for everything, the dark gentleman behind the counter frowned and did a quick monetary conversion on a note-pad. Then he told me that the ice cabinet was outside.

"Did ya get ripped off?" Dick stood by the open car-door while I dumped ice into the new cooler.

"I don't think so. Terry can figure it out. A dollar and eight cents Canadian per U.S. dollar. And what? Two liters to a gallon, roughly?"

"What the hell *was* that dude?" Andy asked.

"Lot's of refugees in this country," I told him. "From *everywhere*. Hand me some beers."

"All *right*! Now you're talkin'!" Dick said.

He wasn't too happy when I told him: "Not yet. We need to put them on ice awhile first."

The way across southern Ontario on the 402 seemed very long in the middle of the night. The Canadians kept their freeways pristine; few billboards, no clusters of fast-food at every interchange. There were plenty of semis hauling ass for Toronto and points east but few cars at that hour. Terry and I sipped our acrid coffees. I slowed to nurse the gas mileage. As we skirted London, the tank was still three-quarters full. We'd make it to Toronto easily. We'd make it to dawn.

The radio had given out east of the Strathroy exit. When we pulled off for Terry to drive, I thought about the mysterious radio in the trunk. It would surely have an FM setting, as new as it appeared to be. But Andy Ritten was snoring softly and Dick Lester had apparently not taken any of his speeders yet. Slamming the trunk would alert them.

"I'll bet those beers are about right by now," I whispered.

Terry brought us back up to speed and merged behind a flatbed stacked with plywood. "I can wait. Lemme get past Toronto. If I pound a few when we get near the track, maybe I'll be able to sleep."

As I took over the radio, we merged onto the 401. I tried to find something halfway artful to keep my driver entertained. I wasn't going to wait any longer to toast myself. The soft *cush* sound as I pulled the ring tab didn't stir the passengers. The moment wasn't totally momentous, due to my years of debauchery at college, but the beer had a satisfying bite, nevertheless.

"Did Sherman say anything to you about Gwen?"

Terry's silhouette shrugged in the dashboard lights. "Not much. I made him aware that I thought it was a pretty bogus move."

"I *like* the guy. I keep telling myself I'd've probably done the same thing."

"We're pretty much dogs, alright. He seems to regret it, but he hasn't come out and said 'cause he's got a little bit of Billy Badass going on about it."

"He's avoiding *me*," I sighed. I finished off the *Pabst*. I folded the can so it wouldn't roll around on the carpetless floor. "Would *you* drop Gwen? if it was you?"

"Geez, Fritch. I don't know. She's a great looking little ol' gal. Why wouldn't she just dump *you* if she wasn't really sorry?"

"That's what I keep thinking. But how much should you put up with? I hadn't gotten laid in six months, and then I couldn't believe she wanted to go out with *me*."

"It's a mismatch, no argument," Wickersham chuckled. "And now a dilemma for you."

Ahead, the skyline of Toronto began to show. Two eastbound lanes became three, then four. Access lanes fell in with us from the south, the traffic still light at 4:30. The skyscrapers, when we came to them, stayed over on the right-hand side. Descending aircraft added to the light show.

With Toronto behind us, the turn-off for the track wasn't much farther. The sky paled rapidly, a widening rose streak.

"I'll have one now," Terry said.

When I had opened a beer and passed it to him, I cracked another for myself. "We get off in Bowmanville and head north about eight miles. We need to stop somewhere for another cooler and ice. We'll gas up, too."

"Those boogers are zonked *out*." Terry slurped foam. "If *that* doesn't wake 'em."

"We're gonna have to roust them for another contribution."

"I'd almost pay their share just to leave 'em sleep."

I tipped my beer, colder now by two hours on ice. The daylight coming up made me uneasy. It always meant that I'd been up too late--worked too late or partied longer than what made sense. At dawn the hours began to count down toward the start of a shift or a morning class. Better to be dreaming already when daylight probed the drapes.

The main exit at Bowmanville turned out to be the route we needed. The Gulf gas-station was at the bottom of the exit, just where you'd find it in the States. There was a banner on stakes along the median proclaiming: "Welcome Race Fans." The BP plaza across the road had the same one. Terry supervised the fueling while I went in for ice. When I came out with another cheap cooler, Ritten and Lester had stumbled forth to stretch. Terry was exacting another couple of dollars from each.

Dick griped briefly that he hadn't been awakened for the first cold brews. Again, we talked him out of drinking a warm one. We packed six more on ice in each cooler. I climbed back behind the wheel and we headed north.

The day brightened as we wound through the countryside. I knew we were getting close. Many front yards offered stacks of campfire wood to race fans. Dick offered the *Christmas Trees* around. Terry and I declined.

"You know, Dick," I said. "There aren't going to be a lot of people awake to party with, if that's what you're thinking."

"Yeah, I guess. But I slept, what, four hours? I'm good to go."

"I'm ready to crash," Terry said. "You can scout around, get us invited to breakfast."

"Do I need to lock up the beers?" I asked.

"No."

I followed the signs. The road widened to three entrance lanes for Mosport International Raceway. A line of early arriving cars moved slowly through one lane of Goodyear Gate. A car behind us turned off its headlights. One guy outside on our right waved us forward. I rolled the window down for the old gentleman on our left wearing a day-Glo vest. It cost us four dollars apiece for infield admission. I handed him a twenty and got back four Canadian dollar coins, *loonies*, with that mournful bird stamped on them. The guy wasn't doing any rate exchanges with the line growing behind us.

"Just follow this road around to the left 'til you go in the tunnel, ay? Go past the paddock area, then it branches off anywhere you want to go." He tore off four stubs and handed the tickets in. "Enjoy the race."

Inside the gate, three women wearing change-aprons awaited the throngs with stacks of programs. I shelled out two of the *loonies* to get one. We followed the access road to the tunnel then drove under the track. Not too far in, past the garage and paddock area, past long rows of Porta Potties, VIP parking, and concessions tents, the scene resembled Woodstock--if the kids at Woodstock had brought pop-up campers and tents.

The sweet, lingering smoke of campfire embers soon perfumed the car. Here and there, up early or way late, campers trudged along the road. A young woman wrapped in a blanket moved out of our way then turned toward a bank of Potties.

"Was that cannabis we just drove through?" Dick sat up straight and leaned like a spaniel toward Terry's open window.

"I believe you're right," Terry smiled.

"Now I *know* I'm up for all day."

I crept and bounced all the way to the back of the 2.5 mile course. The gravel road became increasingly washboarded and dusty. It climbed over small sandy hillocks, narrowed between tents and vehicles parked at all angles. When the road became a two-track, branching toward a woods on the right and a sea of tents near the track fence on the left, I began looking for a spot to park. Dead ahead, the thin trampled grass fell away to a short back chute. I fit us between a VW Microbus and a Mustang veneered with dust. I could have eased farther down the hill but didn't want to alarm the occupants of two tents in front of those vehicles.

"This'll work." I set the parking brake and turned off the ignition. "We should probably keep our voices down."

As we piled out, I could see pedestrians in the dawn light, already taking advantage of the open track. Streams of joggers, hikers, and bicyclists who hadn't over-indulged in the night, now moved quietly below us in both directions.

I handed Dick and Andy their first beers. "These won't be totally cold yet, but go ahead. You've showed *marvelous* restraint. You want a hamburger?"

They each took one when I unfolded the foil. "I'm gonna walk around," Dick said.

"I'm gonna flake out," Andy said. "Let me get my bag and that radio."

"I *wondered* whose that was." I handed him the trunk key.

"I call back seat," Terry said. "Just lemme hang my feet out the window."

"Put your big ol' head down on the passenger side, OK?" I told him. "I'm gonna see how far this seat folds back."

I rolled the front windows up most of the way and started another beer. The Maverick seat tilted until it touched Terry's legs. I turned the sun visor down but it wasn't going to help for long. I found some dark plastic lenses in the glove compartment and clipped them onto my glasses. My tired eyes closed over a whirl of unprocessed images: My shrinking Gramma, the dusk and weary expectations back in Celeryville; the lead smoke and heat of the taillight torch-solder area at Fisher Body-Pontiac; Gwen astride Steve Sherman; the flashlight of a worn-down border guard; the bar manager giving us a break as he perspired toward a cardiac event; just enough gas station coffee for an all-nighter without an exam at the end; the beers to ration. A year ago, I was still borrowing the family's back-up Rambler Classic to go to my summer job at the pickle factory. Now I was the captain of a major road trip. No more calling home for roadside assistance.

I guess I dozed. The voice in the shallow dream was probably just the PA announcer saying good-morning to the campers. He talked softly, enumerating a schedule of morning events. My mind was in just deep enough to blend it with other concerns. He spoke about another driver killed in Saturday practice--Dick Brown in a hand-built prototype with a 426 cid engine. Not *our* Dick, tracking down pot fumes. Sometimes you could smell pot on the torch-solder line, underneath the used motor oil we applied to keep our wooden paddles from igniting as we stirred molten lead. The guys in the grinding booth who touched up our work wore full shop-coats and welder's helmets. They were tested every few months for lead poisoning. Never studied *that* in Biology. Terry snored fitfully, snarling into alarming pauses. You never smelled *bacon* in that part of the Body Shop. I heard the tinny clatter of someone's breakfast utensils down the hill. That would explain the bacon.

When I awoke, Terry had somehow wormed his way out the passenger door without disturbing me. He sat smoking, his sleeping bag spread beneath him on the hood of the Maverick. Dick leaned there too, hip-to-hip with a frizzy Canadian teeny-urchin whose face I could not yet judge. I found the lever and let the seat prop me upright with a jolt. A whine of high-pitched engines approached from below and to our left then howled over to the right, under the Uniroyal foot bridge and into the woods.

"Fritch! Get your ass out here! These guys are nuts!"

When I stood up, careful not to ding the Microbus with my door, I had to wait for the furious swarm to come back around. There were no stragglers so whatever preliminary race it was must have just begun. It turned out to be motorcycles with sidecars which I had never witnessed before. The riders hung way out over the side to compensate for g-force exerted in the turns. Shifting body weight, their backs and helmets inches above the asphalt then hurtled up behind the driver, kept the cycle upright and fast through the two corners in our view.

Terry shook his head in disbelief, saving his voice until the piercing racket had gone by.

"Yeah! They're crazy!" I yelled.

Dick's waif would have been cute after an orthodontist and a bath, but I realized that she may have been camping since Thursday. I was glad to see they were sharing one of Dick's beers. The girl finished it for him then fired up a butane lighter under a roach secured in a bobby-pin; *her* dope, apparently.

"Did ya hear a guy got killed yesterday?" Dick asked before holding the roach under his nose.

"I was hoping I dreamt it, but yeah."

"I sure don't wanta see nobody get killed. What a downer, huh?" He handed the remaining ash back to the girl.

Struggling to keep a straight face, Terry said, "They'll fly their flags at half-staff in honor of Dick's killed buzz."

All three burst into laughter, finally gasping until the sidecars came back around. It appeared that Terry had hit the Canadian joint as well.

"Is that what they're gonna do?" I shouted.

"Prob'ly," Terry yelled back, over the also-ran bikes. "Along with some kinda ceremonial pace-lap for that other guy, too. The car builder."

"Where did Andy go?" I fished a beer out of the cooler, and the last hamburger before it slid into the icy water. Suddenly ravenous with a *contact* appetite, I munched it cold, without condiments.

None of them knew. Andy's sleeping bag had been empty when Terry coughed to life. Then Dick wandered back sharing a cardboard tray of french fries with the girl, Rabbit. *They* hadn't seen him. The girl turned out to be partly an *aboriginal person* as Dick explained. "They aren't Indians up here. Especially not *American* Indians."

Rabbit snickered.

"Can we break out the chips?" Terry asked, already digging in the trunk.

"Sure, but I'm going for a walk."

I hoped I could shake the melancholy of caffeinated images from which I'd awakened. There had to be enough pleasant stimuli to do the job if I walked back in the direction we had come. Campfires and Coleman stoves had been rekindled all along the way. Bare-chested males and their tube-topped companions floated Frisbees near the road, stepping aside for vehicles still searching for parking spots. These raised billows of dust as the late arrivals lurched slowly up the two-track. The dust had a baked scent, blending in a potpourri of suntan oil, scattered reefer, and, I presumed, actual Canadian bacon. After a brief pause, the motorcycles were replaced by open-wheeled club racers. For a few minutes, I watched these Formula Fords whine past from a high point in the trail. Then I pressed on, my head on a swivel to spot Andy Ritter. I resisted the notion to call or whistle for him. I would go as far as the first concession stand.

Adulthood must be like Christmas at this stage, I concluded. The holiday always upended me emotionally when it was over--something so long anticipated and then gone in a day. But adulthood would go right on tomorrow. That's where my analogy broke down. Bruce McLaren was gone, but my magazine said that his race-cars would continue to be built. Gwen *wasn't* gone. Maybe I should have a little faith.

I found a breakfast sandwich at that first food place--cheese and a rubbery egg between sheaves of butter-soaked toast. Before I looped into the tent settlement on my left, a sparsely attended phalanx of Porta-Potties presented itself. I used one then resumed my march. Detouring around some whacked-out kids napping in the sun, I arrived near the woods which bordered the long back-stretch. Following this buffer area back to the east soon brought me to another two-track. The Uniroyal Bridge appeared directly in my path so I knew that my friends must be up on the promontory to my left. Andy Ritter was just coming down the bridge steps from outside of Turn 4.

"Whatcha got there?" I called.

Andy saw me and stooped to rest his burden on the ground. "Geez, those got heavy. Long necks. I made a trade. My radio."

The full-sized cases were of *Molson Export* beer. "Andy, you didn't have to do that. It'll take all day and night to finish them and then we have to drive."

He shrugged. "Well, we've got Dick, ya know. Anyway, these kids said they couldn't get great electronics for some reason. Maybe they were just desperate for tunes."

"Yeah, but your *radio*, dude." I couldn't deny that it was going to be a relief not to worry about having enough brews to go around.

"My contribution. Besides," he added with a broadening smirk. "I scored a gram of hash, too. From one of those Pakistanis like in Sarnia. Least that's what the dude said it was."

"I'll let *you* guys to test it."

I hefted one of the beer cases and we trudged up the hill. The PA announcer had begun to call the starting grid for the Can-Am, beginning with the slower machines at the back. We walked along the line of spectator cars facing the short chute until we found my Maverick. Terry had peeled off his shirt and lay sunning on the hood, his sleeping bag spread back to the wipers. Between chugs of *PBR* and tokes, Dick and Rabbit fondled each other on Andy's bedroll. Everyone sprang up to admire Andy's treasures.

"We're gonna need ice pretty soon," Terry advised. "We're down to cold water."

"I saw a booth back by the paddock when we came in."

"I'll go after the start," he volunteered.

Dick examined the crumbs of hashish which Andy displayed, carefully cupping the foil in his palm. "That sure *looks* like hash," was his assessment. "Same oily resins."

The crowd on the hillside slowly stood up from their blankets and lawn chairs when the Canadian Anthem was introduced. There were no flags to face or salute way out at that end of the course. I'd attended enough hockey games to know the lyrics but even Rabbit was too stoned to sing along. We quit talking, at least. Most of the spectators around us remained standing for the command to fire engines. Then we could hear the field from nearly a mile away, the rumble a low, modulated thunder vibrating in our chests.

The plan, according to the PA guy, was for the two McLaren cars on the front row to hang back through most of the pace-lap. Dan Gurney, in the pole position, and the Kiwi driver Denis Hulme on the outside, would honor Bruce and Dick Brown by creeping slowly, far behind the pack. We'd all seen the riderless charger trailing the horse-drawn funeral cortege; or the lone fighter plane breaking formation to burn heavenward.

We had to cover our ears when the pace-car and pack crawled into view. They wove and darted, heating up the oil, the rubber and brakes, before the long chase. Andy gaped. Terry shook his head in awe. Dick and Rabbit could only giggle at the immense and inescapable noise; the complete palette of colors. All manner of older McLarens, Lolas, Porsches, along with BRM, Ti-22, and the radically small wedge of the Shadow made their way through Corner Four then into the woods. When the throbbing of acceleration had rumbled up the back stretch, we dropped our hands from our ears. A great ovation greeted the two trailing orange Team McLaren cars.

"Hey, Fritch! Check it out," Dick chortled. "Hey, Rabbit! Say 'ass!' This is cool!"

The McLarens turned up the wick somewhere on the back stretch to take their rightful place at the front. Rabbit leaned into me, her smile embarrassed or demented, maybe both.

"Go ahead! But I've already heard your 'bean' and 'a-gane' and 'a-boot,'" I told her.

"Well then, have you heard 'ahhsss?'" She giggled, stumbling back against Dick.

I heard the PA shouting that the field had seen the green flag wave and were blasting into Turn One. Then the announcer was drowned out. At that distance the noise, with all the accelerator peddles on the floor, took on the incandescence of a space launch. We covered our ears again, even before they came into view, even with a long way to go.

Prep Work

Marty Boulanger was supposed to help Hector Fritch paint the old house south of the fairgrounds. He and Hector car pooled down to the assembly-line. Now, they were both on strike against GM. Everyone said it was going to be a long one.

Fritch found the painting job through a high-school friend who worked at *Celeryville Hardware*. Rick Bondry knew Fritch was desperate for money and then old Mr. Whitlow asked him if he knew any painters who worked cheap. Rick left a message and the old man's number at Hector's parent's place.

One more day on the damned preparation, and they could get started. That was the part Fritch hated. It looked like the job had been put off since before Korea. The grime was embedded; decades of dust from harness racing and tractor pulls at the fairgrounds. They rented a power washer, but the water pressure at that end of town was lousy. It didn't strip all of the peeling paint. They waited a day for everything to dry out. Marty had some experience painting cars, so he went ahead and masked all the windows. Then he had to take off. He remembered it was his day to sign up for food stamps as the union had advised them.

So, there was still another day's worth of scraping to do. Fritch dragged the extension ladder to the north end of the bungalow. The ladder wasn't run up all the way but still sagged and bounced as he climbed. Reaching up to get the fascia and the soffit underneath was the worst part. Some hornets under there were lethargic in the October chill. He crushed a few with the wide scraper and then cut the small nest loose. At least the house wasn't very high. He wasn't afraid to look down. Some tired leaves fluttered past his shoulder.

Fritch heard Boulanger's 327 Nova from three blocks away. When he twisted around, he could tell that Marty wasn't coming to work. He wasn't wearing his grubby coveralls.

"Hey, man," Marty said.

"What's up?"

"Hey, I got a job."

"Yeah? Lucky you."

"*Grant's Bump Shop.* So, more masking. I start after lunch."

"Wish *I* knew how to do something." Fritch swung back toward the lap siding, reaching way out with the scraper. He would soon need the one he'd screwed to a broom handle.

"Well, you're learning how to paint houses." Marty sipped coffee from a small Styrofoam cup. "I'll owe you part of that deposit back. Say, twenty bucks?"

They had split the hundred dollars Old Man Whitlow gave them to get started. They told him they needed to buy supplies. He made a surly remark to the effect that they didn't seem very professional. Fritch thought Marty was about to tell him to get his wrinkled old ass up the ladder and do it himself. That would have been just like Marty. But they had money in hand and there would be two hundred more when they were done.

"Sounds about right," Hector said. "Can I get it this weekend? The wedding's Saturday. We're keeping it small, but I'm trying to put together a honeymoon. Now I won't get two coats done in time."

Steam rose from Marty's coffee. The sun wouldn't find this side of the house until noon. "Sure. No problem. You in your apartment yet?"

Fritch came down one step. He switched hands to get a blister of paint on the other side. "Almost. We're still cleaning. Place was a wreck, but *I'm* in there."

Marty lit a smoke. He flung a few last drops of coffee onto the ground to use the cup as an ash tray. Old Man Whitlow had warned them about butts in his yard. "The place above *Simmon's Appliance*, right?"

More paint flakes drifted toward the dewy grass. "Yeah. It's an end-to-end deal on the third floor. Just park in the alley. Stairs are in back."

Marty turned back toward his car. "I'll get the money to you," he called. "Sorry to leave you hangin'."

When Fritch came down another step, he could no longer reach the wall. It was time to move the ladder. Thanks a hell of a lot, he thought, as Boulanger rumbled away.

—m—

By the end of the day, Fritch thought he was ready. Once he could just start making fresh white surface, he'd feel like he was getting somewhere. Right now though, the house actually looked worse. It had bare spots all over it like some kind of rash. He worried a little about rolling paint onto the lap siding. There could be runs and drips if he didn't go easy. But with the long handle, he could make time. Then there were at least eight window frames and the entrance trim.

Fritch lifted the extension off its catches and eased it down. He couldn't leave it up because Old Man Whitlow would gripe about insurance liability. He laid the ladder down against the side of the garage. He set the scrapers and wire brush just inside the door. Fritch hadn't seen them leave, but the Whitlow's big old Buick was gone. Must be Bingo Night somewhere. *Good*, because the old bird made Fritch nervous. Worse than a foreman and he'd probably have to hear him bitch about the missing partner. Fritch would just keep quiet and think about the extra share of money.

—m—

When he had trudged up two flights, the apartment was unlocked. Gwen was already there. The scuffed-up kitchen sink was full of sudsy water.

"And how was *your* day, honey?" He embraced her from behind and kissed the nape of her neck. His mimicry of old-married small talk probably went over her head. "What are we cleaning tonight?"

"Cupboards," she sniffled. "Mom bought us some contact paper." She rested her elbows on the sink's rim. She tried to daub her eyes with her sleeve. The top of the yellow latex glove wasn't very absorbent.

"Hey, what's the matter, baby?" Fritch tightened his grasp on her hips. For a moment, she pressed back against him.

"Howie Titus says I've gotta be in the kitchen, starting tomorrow." Gwen sighed heavily, moving some of the long, dark hair that closed in on her face.

"I'm *showing* too much. I knew this would happen. Hell, if I can't even stay in school, how can I wait on the good citizens of Celeryville?"

Fritch kissed her neck again. "Screw 'em. The whole dining public. If we weren't so poor right now, you could tell the Titus brothers to shove it, too. They're gonna turn you into a libber."

Gwen sniffed with finality and stood up straight. "It's OK. They're being good to me, finding stuff for me to do. It's just my hormones going crazy. My tits are even ahead of my belly."

Fritch moved his hands up. "Don't think I haven't noticed."

Gwen pressed against him again. "Careful with that."

Fritch stepped back. "Let me get washed up then we'll make everything sparkle. Is there anything to eat?"

Gwen pulled the drain stopper. She peeled the gloves off. "Some fries and two grilled cheese somebody didn't pick up. It's already in foil. We can see if the oven works. I bought baloney and a loaf of bread out of my tips."

"Great. Even though we no longer *live* on bread alone," Fritch joked from the echoing bathroom. "Geez, I think the rust in this tub is here to stay. I put this *Comet* down last night." When Gwen didn't respond, Fritch added: "Is *Hillbilly Bread* still pretty cheap?"

—⚏—

Warming the food took awhile. The oven needed a serious cleaning, but it worked. A thin haze of smoke curled down the hallway.

"Wow, what' s burning? Smells like rodent."

"It's too charred to see *what's* in there. The little bulb is burned out too." Gwen measured and cut the contact paper, a dark avocado color. She stood on a chair pulled from the furnished dinette set. The vinyl seat had been patched with duct tape.

When the water finally got hot, Fritch scrubbed and rinsed the tub. There were plenty of rags but only the one wash-cloth and towel he'd brought from home. They were counting on the wedding reception for more. The water pressure was low here, too. Well, it was an old building and up on the third floor. He rinsed with a drinking glass that refilled slowly. Maybe the hard-water stains were a *shade* paler.

"Oh, damn it!" Gwen cried.

"What happened?" Fritch tried to rinse out his rag. Now the water was scalding.

"I left a wrinkle. Should I try to peel it back off?"

"Is it gonna tip over a few plates? Why bother?" He draped the rag over the edge of the tub and shut off the light.

Gwen made a quick measurement of the next shelf then climbed down. "And we don't have an oven mitt."

Fritch rummaged in the utensil drawer. He'd already bought a spatula so he could fry himself an egg. There was a stirring spoon, too, and a corroding ladle they hadn't thrown out yet. "I'll drag it out of there somehow. I'm starving. I already boiled my fingers anyway. *Never* get in that tub without testing the water."

They ate the fries and grilled cheese on paper plates. It was plenty. *Titus Family Restaurant* fries were thick-cut on the premises. Gwen hadn't told him the grilled-cheese were on Texas toast. The oven was hot enough to re-melt the cheese around the edges. There were dill spears included. They fit their dirty plates into a garbage bag by the stairwell. They were hoping the reception would also provide a kitchen waste basket.

"What's next for you?" Gwen asked.

Fritch pushed in his chair. "Dump some bleach in the toilet first. Then I'm gonna make up a bucket and try to swab under the bed."

"Well, be careful."

"I *told* you there's nothing living under there. I got all the coat hangers I could reach. There weren't any in the closet but about a hundred under the bed. And an old slipper. You need the mop yet?"

Gwen rolled out another piece of contact paper on the dinette. She used the metal yard-stick to hold it. "It's all yours. I've gotta do three more pieces of this."

Back in the bathroom, Fritch poured bleach into the darkly stained bowl to let it sit. He filled the bucket with bleach and water so hot it made the old pipes clank and keen. He had just gotten into position to crawl under the bed with the mop and flashlight when Gwen came down the hall. He heard a zipper and the waitress uniform hitting the floor. She paused in the bedroom door to step out of her panties.

"Right now?" Fritch raised up, nearly bonking his head on the bed-frame.

"I *told* you. *Crazy.*" She flopped backward onto the open sleeping bag he'd been using. "Please come up here?"

Fritch unbuckled and kicked his jeans aside. "I haven't had a bath. Why don't you just stay over?"

"My folks are pissed off enough already," Gwen said. Her eyes were closed. "I need that...that thing we do. *You* do. You don't hardly need to get me ready, but...I *love* that anyway."

Fritch tossed his briefs. He left his socks on. He didn't know yet that it was considered classless. He never minded this part. Luckily, he *had* learned there was more to pleasing a woman than simply jabbing away. Too bad it wasn't a paying occupation. Gwen had only *heard* about it; the rumors and speculations of her friends. She had not experienced anyone's mouth down there before he showed her. "Perfect. That makes us *compatible*," he told her. "Just like it says in Playboy Forum."

Gwen whimpered: "Sure, sure. Just be quiet and get..."

Hector lifted her hand out of the way. He kissed the two fingers she had touched herself with. They usually played in the dark so her glistening folds were a surprise. He sensed that this wasn't going to take long. He tasted tentatively and then licked slowly 'round her pronounced button. He hoped *that* taste wasn't about to change. When would they have to quit for a while? The sixth month? The seventh? That should be *her* area of expertise.

The whimpering became guttural. Her swelling abdomen was still taut with most of her cheerleader muscle tone. She began to arch. He was pleased but almost embarrassed that he could have such an effect with so little effort. He closed his eyes too and tried not to make any friction against the lumpy mattress. First things first.

He needed a distraction. So, but what if his brush strokes tomorrow could be long and insistent as well? Or, then gentle and daubing. The tips of the bristles finding every cranny and ridge of the entrance frame. Slow and delicate along the caulk bead. Then broader, pushing the paint out thickly onto the sill. Shift the ladder to stroke the shutter slats and the head jamb. Persist, even when his arm gets weary. Make sure it's completely done before he climbs down. Someone will shout. Probably to get his attention and tell him *good job*. Then he'll step back to admire it himself.

The Pot-Luck Wedding Reception Blues

I suppose we were fortunate to have a reception of any kind. Even the following day, in the multi-purpose room rented from *Sacred Heart* church. The quickie wedding itself took place at *St. Paul Lutheran* where Gwen used to go. Parents and siblings only; a Maid-of-Honor and a Best Man. And the best man was my brother. Two birds with one stone. Well, like I said, we were lucky to have even *that* with a minimum of animosity on everyone's part. Gwen should have been a senior at Celeryville High and was already starting to show. I was a college drop-out on strike at General Motors, bringing home $25 a week. The plan was to get the ceremony done, throw together a reception the next day when the hall was available; then, picket duty on Monday morning at Pontiac Motors. At least a reception and some odd-job money allowed me to go out on the precarious financial limb of a night out. So, I have to describe how we spent the night between the Fritch-Deal nuptials and that pot-luck gathering.

I had already thrown down my life's savings for a security deposit plus first month's rent of an apartment above an appliance repair place in Celeryville. That sum represented the pitiful scrapings of someone who'd spent a year of bachelor hedonism since landing the assembly-line job. But with congratulatory cash anticipated, some of which would go for rent, there was no reason not to have at least a one-night honeymoon. My dad had slipped me a twenty. So had the Best Man, home on leave from the Air Force. It was Sweetest Day, after all. The very first one, I believe. *I'd* sure never heard of it before. I remembered to hoist ol' Gwen over the threshold. We ditched our dress-up-like-adults clothing at the apartment.

"But we need a decent floor lamp," Gwen said. "And we won't eat much without a toaster oven."

"Somebody'll bring us a lamp. Count on it," I assured her. So we ignored the piles of hand-me-down household crap left to be put away and hit the road for Port Huron.

Coney-dogs, chili, and a pitcher of draft at the *Brass Rail* would have been good enough for me. It was one of my favorite joints from my student days at Port Huron College. But, as we cruised into town, I also noticed the marquis in front of McMorran Arena. The local hockey team, the *Flags*, were hosting Dayton later that evening.

"The *Flags* are in town," I said.

"I see that," Gwen admitted in a neutral tone. "It's always so cold in there."

Well, maybe if I let her pick the restaurant. I was quickly formulating a theory of matrimonial give-and-take. Compromise. I motored past the *Rail*, north up Pine Grove Avenue, looking for a classy steak house or something with their name on a matchbook that Gwen could put in our wedding album. The scenario of going to a minor league hockey game on our wedding night, and especially relating the story later, was just too sweet to dismiss. It was time for our first bargain, beginning with a decent meal.

The late afternoon dinner rush at *Kogan's* was just starting. Gwen shrugged and didn't have any huge objections when I pressed her about the hockey game, even though *Kogan's* wasn't exactly five-star dining. It was a family place and the families looked like *they* were headed to the *Flags* game. I don't think Gwen was that interested in a big first-night sexual extravaganza either. We would have been hard pressed, at that point, to come up with anything new to try in the sack, though we would certainly struggle to expand our repertoire later. What irritated Gwen *more* was that I didn't think it was a good idea for her to order an alcohol beverage. The new, plain wedding band had not added any years to her cheerleader face. The wait staff might not serve *me* if I was clearly in there with a minor. I convinced her to order a soda and promised to pour her some of my pitcher on the sly.

The steaks weren't too bad and they brought my *Strohs* in a frosted schooner glass. Gwen would have ordered ground sirloin, but I reminded her that we might be eating beanie-weenies next week. We waited for hers to be *well-done*.

When we rolled back downtown, I discovered that the parking lot of *Blue Water Motor Lodge* was nearly filled. My heart sank as I dashed in to the reservation desk. It turned out that the *Dayton Gems* had brought quite a fan following. The *Blue Water*, just a block from the arena, was apparently tolerant of Booster Club excesses. The team was staying overnight there, as well, before bussing on to Saginaw and Muskegon.

Luckily, there were two rooms left, though neither happened to be the Honeymoon Suite. I paid for the single king-size then went back out with the glad tidings. Gwen carried her tackle-box of make-up and I dragged in our lone suitcase. After we'd turned on the television, run the shower a short burst, inventoried the free toiletries, and peeked into the mini-bar, Gwen announced it was time for a quick nap. She really meant *nap* and was soon snoring softly. I groped around in the mini-bar and found a small bottle of domestic champagne. I ignored the exorbitant $8 price tag, which would come out of my phone deposit at check-out. The principle of steak-instead-of-ground sirloin still seemed to apply. Well, I'd pour Gwen one, too, before we walked over to the game. I threw the wire into the trash and wrenched the plastic stopper out with my teeth. I hit it straight from the bottle. It could have been colder, I thought, for the price.

The game was alright, even though the *Flags* lost by two goals. It was loud in there, with lots of almost good-natured taunting between the two fan-bases. At least with the place packed, it was a little warmer than usual. And, there were plenty of good scraps on the ice--cathartic for everyone, I supposed. The Port Huron fans went home sated, if not victorious. The Dayton fans headed for the bars or took their carousing straight back to the motel.

Gwen and I took a shower together, just to speed things up in the morning. So, *that* was a first. We took the rest of the champagne in with us. After toweling off, she didn't bother with her new special-occasion teddy, but crawled straight in between the sheets. Maybe we could have had some fun then, but I took the time to let the steam clear from the mirror so I could shave. And, then, what the hell--why not sample one of those imported beers out of the mini-bar? In for a penny, in for a pound. By the time my face was stubble-free, ol' Gwen was once again in dreamland. Geez, and she hadn't really gotten much of that bubbly. When I spooned up to her, she groaned and rolled away. I listened to the elevator bring up the happy *Gems* and more of their boisterous followers; footsteps running or staggering in the hall; keys in tumblers; doors closing; far-away muted laughter. I sipped my *Beck's* in the dark and listened for a long time.

When I woke up, it just didn't seem right, not to have sex at least once on our ersatz honeymoon. I got up and went to the bathroom first. Gwen didn't have any aspirin in her purse. I resumed spooning up against her, sun already slanting through a gap in the curtains. I gave the whole production about fifteen minutes then threw my clothes on to go find some coffee. They had an urn down in the lobby. I settled our bill while Gwen dressed and packed.

Bleary-eyed hockey players were gathering for the Continental breakfast when we came down through the lobby. Gwen took the car keys and the suit-case while I refilled two more coffees and grabbed us a couple of donuts. The big *Indian Trails* bus was warming out in the lot. That must be a cool life, I thought; to be young and have a particular talent. But wasn't *I* young? Something cold but brief pulsed below my sternum. Then we were on our way back to Celeryville with only church traffic to contend with.

It was almost eleven a.m. when we tromped up the back staircase to our rail-road flat. I gulped a couple of aspirin from the sparsely stocked medicine cabi-net. I washed them down with my last *Strohs* longneck out of the nearly barren refrigerator. It was one of those relic models with the cooling element on top like a spool for telephone wire. The light was burned out but I could see our *Tabasco* and mustard in the door; some kind of foil shrouded leftover from *Titus Family Restaurant* where Gwen worked.

The reception wasn't going to be one of those fancy catered affairs where everyone munches peanuts and mints while the newlyweds finish their photo shoot. Gwen's mom had made it clear that Gwen would be expected to help set up and I wanted to make sure my stereo was placed for optimum effect. I still had the little dorm-room turntable with detachable speakers. There wasn't going to be a DJ either; not even *me* if I stuck to the business of being sociable to strangers. I had to find someone I could trust to select the right tunes.

"Do I need a tie again?" I called from the bedroom, way at the end of the hall. I took my light blue dress shirt off its hanger and sniffed the armpits. I might have been just a little nervous at the ceremony yesterday.

Gwen had taken my place in front of the yellowing bathroom mirror. "You better. Everyone'll want pictures."

I walked back down the long hallway, loosening the noose of my one decent tie. "Well, did you save your bouquet? I didn't see it in the fridge."

"Ma's got it," Gwen said, making smoochy lips with a fresh application of very red lipstick. She had great fashion sense, for a kid. Her dress was a deep purple crushed velvet. Not quite a mini, but mid-thigh, anyway. She'd found matching heels.

"What *is* that in there?" I asked.

"What's *what* in where?"

"The leftovers in the fridge."

"Meatloaf sandwich," she said, reaching for the big alligator-jaws curling thingy. "That bread'll be soggy."

I put my hand on her hips just as she lifted the device toward her bangs. "Look out," she warned me in the mirror.

"So? You want half?"

She sighed, glancing down at her tummy, already threatening the fit of the dress. "Yeah. Yeah, I could eat."

I don't really need any other condiments if I have my *Tabasco*. We were going to have to invest in some mayo, though. The bread didn't want to come off of Gwen's half in one piece but I managed to smear a little mustard under there. I left it on the foil for her and went to eat over the sink. There was a fine view of grimy brick wall out the window.

"Now I'll have to do my lipstick again," she said, plucking up the sandwich. "We've gotta get moving or Ma'll be pissed."

"Bruff our teef firft," I mumbled. "Those are some really sticky lips for kissing all those aunts and grannies," I noted after swallowing.

She tried to bite off small nibbles but it didn't work. "I know. But it's for the pictures. Don't you like 'em?"

"Oh, yeah. I like 'em fine."

She put her crusts back on the foil and returned to the bathroom. I followed her, then took my toothbrush out to the kitchen sink. Gwen was focused on her make-up again so she didn't notice as I squeezed the toothpaste directly into my mouth. It was another bachelor habit I'd have to grow out of. But on our reception day, it was just another pet peeve I'd planted that would gestate later.

"We better take both cars," I told her. "To haul home all the loot."

Most of the cast from the wedding were already at the *Sacred Heart* Community Hall when we arrived. My mother rolled out the white paper table coverings. A couple of my new brothers-in-law were unfolding chairs. Bernice, my mother-in-law, poked at a couple of hams in the kitchen. Gwen headed back there. Her mother pointed out the veggies to be chopped and sliced. I could see the candles already fired up under serving pans on the buffet table. The two grandads-to-be were pooling their knowledge of hydraulics over the pump assembly of a beer keg in the bar alcove.

"Patrick's not here yet?" I asked my mother.

"He was just getting out of the shower when we left." She had begun distributing centerpieces of plastic autumn flowers and wedding bells.

"But he's *coming*, right?"

"Well, of course. I think he's still researching your toast. Why?"

I made a closer inspection of the room. Sure enough, there was a small stage in a rear corner. Probably where they set up the bingo hopper. "He's got my stereo in the back of his car."

Bernice came out of the kitchen with another chafing dish for the buffet. "I can't believe that wasn't your first piece of *furniture!*"

I scratched my head. "Yeah, I don't know what I was thinking. We've been running in and out of there so we didn't need it."

"But *now* you wanta watch all us old folks dance?"

I headed toward the tapper room where the dads had drawn off a first pitcher of foam. I could certainly wait for it to settle. "Yikes," I called back. "I didn't think about *that* either."

"We don't want it loud," my mother warned. "People will want to chat. We all want to talk about *you*."

The guests began to arrive early because the guests were catering the event. Gwen had about a hundred aunts, uncles, and cousins from up in the Thumb. Like her dad, most of them were farmers or dairymen working for other farmers. Lots of flat-top haircuts and hay-baling tans, corn-on-the-cob bellies. Bernice had been on the phone a lot in the past week, so most of the women carried casserole dishes. A couple of sturdy men-folk from Caro supported Gwen's ancient grandmother across the parking-lot by her elbows.

My family rolled in, too. Skilled trades uncles including electricians like my dad. A few of my cousins had been in this same domestic situation so their best wishes were empathetic. Gwen's Maid-of-Honor made a clamorous entrance along with a few other girlfriends from work. Robin Hebert was always ready to party. She pinned on the corsages and collected the first pitcher for the wedding party--not counting the one I carried in my left hand so I could greet guests with my right. I heard Patrick's Camaro Z-car rumbling its glass-packed mufflers outside. He lugged the stereo in and set it up where I pointed. He went back out for a stack of LPs, but my mother intercepted him. She handed him some old favorites from home.

"Put *these* on while we eat," she told him, her jaw set in no-nonsense profile. The newest things they owned were *The Association* and *The Mamas and the Papas*, which I had abandoned to them and which I immediately prayed to hear. Then *Herb Alpert and the Tijuana Brass* came on, low and tinny like elevator music.

At a pause in the arrivals, I sipped from the pitcher and wandered over to the windows. Where were *my* friends--besides at far-flung campuses and in the jungles of Southeast Asia? Since quitting college, I'd found myself allied with the younger, street-corner-hippy vanguard that had taken root in our little community. Several of these self-styled *freaks* represented, for me, a pale facsimile of what passed for a counter-culture at Port Huron College. They'd never heard of Kafka or Camus, but they wore the same surplus military garb, faded bell-bottom jeans, and raggedy sneakers or boots. They drank beer in the back seats of clunker cars on the way to rock concerts and bragged of smoking more Michigan ditch-weed than I'd ever seen them score. But a few of them turned out to be the kind of buds who usually had my back. They were always up for any kind of cheap thrills or road-trips. So where *were* they? I hadn't told anyone that the event required formal attire.

"We're gonna eat." Gwen took hold of my elbow and turned me toward the short table reserved for the wedding party. She stopped me long enough to pin on my boutonniere, also salvaged from yesterday. I wasn't much help with that pitcher in my hand. How had they kept the beer so cold? Maybe Gwen's dad had stashed it in the milking parlor. The veins in my head dilated, the new alcohol washing my old hangover onto a back burner.

"*Shall* we pray?" Pastor Bettner had showed up, too, though I thought his duties were completed with yesterday's solemnities. He wore horn-rimmed glasses but had a voice that belonged on late-night FM radio.

We were first in the serving line. Well, *that* was a perk. Now we heard Patti Page or Rosemary Clooney--some fifties torch stuff on the stereo. Robin yakked on and on as she loaded her plate. After a few drinks she was leaning in, getting right in Patrick's face, though I think one of his girl friends was sitting out with the groundlings. "Aren't you glad to be *home*?" "I *love* your car." "It's cool they don't make you shave your head like in the Marines."

Gwen took ham, salad, and two species of green bean casserole. "No scalloped potatoes, baby. Are you *watching* this? No roll, either. All this food is ridiculous." She led the way to our seats. I arranged my own mountain of unfamiliar victuals then headed toward the bar to top off our beer. The silverware began to clatter, so I went back and quickly kissed her over her violet shoulder.

The place was soon loud enough to drown out the Korean War music. Lots of folks talking and chewing at the same time. There were skilled trenchermen in both families. Of course the clans gravitated to their own tables. There hadn't been time to plot a seating arrangement. I doubted if many of them would ever see each other again. I'd only been to one Deal family picnic. Our own family reunions were less frequent as my cousins married and spread out. No, now wait a second, I thought. What about a baptism for ol' Ziggy zygote in there, fighting for space against Gwen's second plateful? Nah. Well, the *grand-parents* would be there, for sure.

Patrick and I had just drained the last of my second pitcher when Bernice stepped between my seat and Gwen's. "Time to circulate," she told Gwen. "While everyone's sitting, so you don't miss anybody."

As I stood up, steadying myself on the back of the folding chair, I discovered my mother lurking as well. "Ease off on the beer," she said.

"Are you counting?"

"Yes, I *am*. You're going to cut the cake in a few minutes, and I don't want you face down in it."

Gwen decided to pile on: "*I* get to do that, right?"

"Yup, and we still have *lots* of pictures to take," Mom added. "Your nose already looks like a tomato." She and Bernice went to find their cameras.

I guess I managed to fake sobriety throughout the schmoozing. Each table offered at least one chair-back to lean on--men gone to the bathroom or after more beer and grub; children excused to chase and skate around on the polished tiles. I tended not to be a very noisy drunk, especially among strangers. Maybe I didn't make *too* bad an impression on Gwen's people. My own aunts and uncles probably *knew* better. Anyway, they'd held back their ribbing long enough, the essence of which was that I must not be gay after all. I just took it with a smile. I may have reminded some of them about their *own* glass houses. Younger souls commandeered the music. Three middle-school girls I didn't recognize started the dancing with some *Zeppelin*. I doubted whether *that* would be tolerated for long. Again, my gaze drifted to the parking-lot in search of my ragamuffin, so-called friends.

Then Patrick chimed his glass to breech the din for his toast. I gratefully returned to the Table of Honor where he filled our glasses with an unfortunate introduction of more domestic champagne. That's probably where everything started to go wrong. The volume of spirits was already greater than last night, the ratio of champagne approaching critical mass. Patrick said something in verse about there being a lot of bees procreating because we'd gathered so many *sons-of-bees* in the place. I wish I could remember it exactly. Everyone laughed. The banging silverware demanded more kissing. Gwen's mouth tasted salty and sweet, of ham and booze. This provoked an unexpected impulse to head back to the apartment, or maybe even just out to the parking lot. But *that* would have been totally rude, so I let it go. Next thing I knew, we were smearing that cake on each other's faces.

After cleaning up the mess, the flash-cubes began popping in front of the gift table--me with all the grandmas; Gwen with several generations of moms, grandmas, and aunts--every possible combination. Patrick was also weaving as he refilled my glass. Robin disappeared for awhile into the women's bathroom. Gwen admired our new lamp--not a floor model, but a nice, buffed-silver looking table lamp to sit on our bedside milk-crates.

I told her that if I was going to help open gifts, I'd need a chair. She wanted one, too. The mothers-in-law passed the packages to us and kept notes. I watched Gwen carefully slice the envelopes. She put the checks and bills back into each one. I don't know why she didn't just stash the dough in her purse. I tried to keep a mental tally. I made it through one month's rent and then lost focus. It was all I could do not to rest my face down on that cool, white paper. Patrick dragged a chair up next to me. He touched a fresh pitcher to the side of my neck. Only the kids were dancing. Their parents began to drag them toward the cloak-room; respects paid, obligations fulfilled. Aunts hugged Gwen. Departing cousins patted me on the back, perceptively advising me not to get up.

The sun was setting, red through the leaf-smoke evening. It flared through the gold and russet foliage of the *Sacred Heart* neighborhood. It reflected off my lime-green *Maverick* as Patrick helped me stack gifts in the back seat. We carried more stuff out to Gwen's old Ford *Galaxy*. Feeble as it may have been, I wanted my stereo back at the apartment. But those same three girls and a few little kids continued to boogie. Jimi Hendrix sawed at the *Sears and Roebuck* speakers. Stragglers, but who's were they? The hall had nearly emptied. My Dad swept the bar alcove then he and Patrick carried out the empty keg. My father-in-law had left at milking time, carting home Gwen's five quarreling sibs. OK. Two lady friends of my mother's still toiled in the kitchen along with Bernice and an aunt from Gwen's side. Or, maybe the little rockers had come in off the street--clever crashers everyone would assume were relatives from the other side.

"Do you have garbage pick-up yet?" My mother called through the serving window.

"I dunno." I plopped down where Gwen was fitting various kitchen devices into a single cardboard box. She stripped off the wrapping paper and wadded it into a *Hefty* bag. "We've got a couple of burn barrels by the alley."

"Well, *Sacred Heart* wants us to dispose of our own trash, so…" My mother emerged from the kitchen with a full garbage bag in each hand.

"OK. I'll wedge it in somehow. I've got a load ready to go so I'm gonna take off."

"You're going?" Gwen pouted, packing her trash down.

"Well," I paused. It might not be the right time to admit how desperately I needed a nap. "I can start putting stuff away," I nimbly rationalized.

She lifted the box of canisters and can-openers into my arms. "Yeah? Start with *these*. I'll be along when we're done." She knotted the *Hefty*. She dragged it and the kitchen bags like Santa Claus near the end of his trip.

"I can come back for those."

"It's fine," she said. "I need some air."

Behind us, my mother nagged: "Are you OK to drive?"

I pretended not to hear as I held the door for Gwen. "Don't forget the stereo," I told her. "And lots of left-overs."

—m—

I took the back streets, easing up to each stop sign. At that hour on a Sunday, Celeryville Police Department had no cruiser on duty anyway. Lapeer County might send a patrol car through later, but he wouldn't make a side-trip into the neighborhoods. The park bench on an empty plot between *Jewel Pharmacy* and *Simmons' Kitchen and Appliance* was deserted. All the freaks were home watching football or recovering from the weekend.. I turned into the alley next to the drugstore then made a left into the parking spaces allowed for nearby apartments.

I wanted to climb those stairs and collapse on the beat old couch which had come *furnished*. But, I'd have to make at least one trip so I might as well make it count. I could manage the lamp in one hand and grip the box of kitchen stuff in the crook of my other arm. Then I'd have to set everything down on the landing to use my key. The evening had turned cool, maybe bracing enough to revive me for a little longer.

The trash had to come out before I could get at the gifts. When I opened the car door, I could smell the trash barrel smoldering. Kind of a bummer after the perfume of leaf smoke. Neighbors on the third floor must have used it.

I didn't know if *Jewel Pharmacy* was even open on Sundays, but I thought it was their barrel too. The neon of *Sam's Party Store* still glowed across the street, and I remembered I was out of beer.

I leaned on the hood of the *Maverick* and undid Gwen's bag of crumpled gift wrap. I could save the bag and the paper would catch easier. It was nearly dark in the notch of the alley. A security light behind the drugstore came on as the flames began to crackle. The streetlights on Capac Avenue didn't reach far into the alley. When the fire took hold, I added one bag of garbage. I hoped there were enough of the fancy paper plates in there to stoke it. A whiff of ham-fat masked the melting bisqueen.

As I was about to feed in the third bag then ascend to my nap, a figure strolled toward me from the opposite end of the alley. "What'cha doin' there, bub?"

Now the fire cast our shadows against the grubby brick of my building. There was no mistaking the silhouette of Terry Wickersham--tall, and draped in an old Air Force dress coat, sans insignia. Above the spacious pockets and pouches, his curly mop of hair spilled down to the epaulettes.

"Gonna make S'mores," I growled. "Where's the *Datsun*?"

He dug in one of the deep pockets for his cigarettes and lighter. "I stopped in to see Dickie Lester about money he owes me and the damn thing wouldn't start. He didn't have any jumper cables, of course."

I used a length of straightened coat-hanger left dangling from the lip of the barrel to poke at the burbling garbage. "*Imagine* that. Told you to buy American."

Terry lit a cigarette. "The old man got it at a wholesale auction. Not every-body's got a great job like you do." He puffed in silence for several minutes. "S'mores, huh? You catch a buzz somewhere?"

I snorted and re-hung the wire. "Yeah, we had a regular Woodstock over at *Sacred Heart.*"

We both stared into the flames and paper embers. Melting plastic forks and wax paper added strange hues in the center of the conflagration. The food scraps and ribbon burned better than I expected. It reminded me of the sum-mer bonfires we'd enjoyed at the abandoned township gravel-pit; the hours of amphetamine babble and beery philosophy--times you never think to squeeze until way later.

"I'm *sorry*, dude," he said, finally.

"Well, geez…I mean, where the hell *was* everyone?"

Terry shook his head. "You can't rely on most of those assholes. I *planned* to come over, but…you *know* your ma doesn't like me."

"Oh, for Chrissake." I scowled. "She doesn't like *any* of my friends. That's practically her *job*."

"She goes on and on about my coat."

"She was *way* too busy for that, believe me."

"And my *hair*, of course. I don't know. And the old man had stuff for me to do in the resale shop 'til after three."

"It wasn't my *mother* getting married! How many times am *I* ever gonna get married?"

Something burst in the heart of the inferno, sending up a short geyser of sparks. Who knew what chemical by-products and out-dated drugs had been cooking in there?

"Remains to be seen," Terry sighed. "Anyway, I feel bad about missing it. That make ya happy?"

I took up the poker again by its cool end. I stirred deep--carbon-crispy sheaves disintegrating into ash. "It helps," I chuckled.

Just then Gwen turned in. The *Galaxy* skidded to a halt behind flying gravel as we scurried out of the way.

"Woah, hey!" Terry exclaimed. "Maybe *she* won't be so easy."

The driver's door flew open and Gwen wriggled out from behind the wheel. "What are you *doing*?!" She cried.

"What's it look like? Look who showed up."

"*Terrific*. But, I think we're missing some money. Some envelopes. Why would you…? Couldn't this wait 'til morning?" She crowded up to the fire and we all peered in.

"It was already going so I…! I didn't *see* anything! I thought you had them all in one stack. They were next to the smaller boxes."

Gwen sniffed and shook her head. "The moms kept track. I've got twenty-two envelopes and they say there should be twenty-five. They had it written down."

I laid my arm over her shoulder. The flames settled lower. You could see a sediment of blackened cans and what appeared to be charred baby-food jars.

Nothing could have survived, unless someone gave us coins. "How much could it have been? I think we *still* did OK."

"I didn't add it up. I headed home as fast as I could."

Now Terry dug into one of his deep pockets. He lifted out the bent, red envelope of a *Hallmark* card and handed it to Gwen. "I *planned* to come," he repeated.

"Wow, check it out," I said. "Maybe we need to keep the reception going for this guy. I was just thinking about walking over to *Sam's.*"

"Well, there's lots of ham and dabs of casseroles, but *I'm* going to bed," Gwen handed Terry's card to me.

"And *I've* gotta get my butt out to Vlasic in the morning," Terry said. "Maintenance is putting on a fall paint shift. I need a ride and I thought you might be interested too."

We all leaned in as the last orange glow withered out of the trash. Three envelopes. Maybe. We'd be able to figure out whose, easily enough. And how many bucks we'd lost. It might not make that big of a difference if the strike could be settled soon. I tended to be optimistic, whether drinking, hung-over or in between. "I'll just get six then. I can drop you off, but then I've gotta go down and picket. You can bring me an application."

Gwen went back to her car for her purse. Terry wasn't old enough to be with me if I was buying alcohol so she loaded him up with a few boxes.

"Make me a sandwich, will ya?" I thumbed a ten out of Terry's card and pushed it deep into my wallet.

"Yeah, but see if they've got any mayonnaise."

"And horseradish," Terry called as I walked toward the lights of the main street. "You've gotta have horseradish."

A Hot Hand

Hector Fritch was no longer drowsy by the time Gwen fell asleep. It was unnecessary to fake sleep after her hand dropped away from his crotch. Her arm, and then the rest of her, slowly rolled over until she faced the window above a narrow space between the older downtown buildings. Some neon from the pool hall across the front street still made it up to the third floor. It glowed through the ratty lace curtains. Yes, she was definitely mouth-breathing--heavily, regularly--her heated, hormonal pulse slowing. Hector risked his way up onto one elbow and peered over the mound of her figure. Hers was, in spite of its pregnant glow, definitely a face in the repose of sleep. He resisted stroking her hair or pulling the quilt higher over her shoulder in consolation of his failed libido. He eased his feet over the high side of the worn, concave mattress. He paused in the doorway, sensing that he'd forgotten some critical detail of this escape. Or was it something else? Another chore he'd neglected? But the uneasiness passed.

Hector crept down the chilly hallway, past the hard water hues of the bathroom and a smaller bedroom they had designated for a nursery. Gwen remained undisturbed as the floorboards creaked. She did not call out to ask where he was fleeing. He had out-waited her but was now wide awake and would have to entertain himself quietly. The only all-night television station they could pick up, from the building's tilted antenna, showed reruns of *Mayberry RFD*.

Hector found the ancient floor lamp that came with their *furnished* front room. He turned the switch once, twice, and then had to repeat the process when a burned-out bulb in the third socket plunged the room back into darkness. He pulled his old college briefcase out from under a couch that rested on two lengths of 4x4 in lieu of the stubby legs missing from its frame. The briefcase rattled like a maraca as he placed it beneath the lamp. He squatted on the avocado carpet, tilting his ear toward the hallway, just to make sure. The radiator next to the television clattered listlessly.

Inside the briefcase, the United States Basketball League waited to play the opening games of its schedule. This was already the week before Halloween and Hector wanted to start at the same time as the other pro leagues. Since the workers at *Fisher Body-Pontiac* plant had gone out as part of a nationwide strike, he'd spent the last two weeks putting rosters together. The summer-long bargaining with General Motors failed just about the same time he and Gwen decided they'd better get married. They still had wedding money, maybe enough for two months rent. There were only a few odd jobs after the seasonal rush at the pickle factory in *Celeryville* ended. He wasn't ready to hunt beer bottles yet after doing one house-painting job. It was too late to pick up a class at the community college over in Flint. He was supposed to be taking a few semesters off, anyway, to get used to married life and then parenthood. Picket duty once each week still left him with too much time on his hands. Managing the league was probably better than watching game shows or pissing his strike benefit away at a tavern down the block.

Hector laid out the eight rosters he had printed on three-by-five cards. He had awarded franchises to cities that didn't have any major professional sports that he knew of. There were just eight teams in case he went back to the assembly-line soon. He could hold an owner's meeting later to expand to two more worthy cities, depending on the economy. He congratulated himself for coming up with some cool team names. The Wheeling, W.VA. *Miners* and Lexington, KY *Long Rifles* were his favorites after the hometown Flint *LeSabres*. He hadn't designed any logos yet. It took all his time to find players out of the newspaper who'd been dropped by the pros during training camp. Then he pored over some old preview magazines to find college seniors who'd been overlooked in the draft. He found local, *regional* picks for each of his teams.

None of these imaginary duties could be done until Gwen left for her job at the restaurant. It was hard to picture her scrubbing pots and pans after the owner of *Titus Family Restaurant* relegated her to the kitchen. Hard for him to imagine her as anything other than a knock-out waitress or hostess. But none of her uniforms fit anymore. Even the fashionable maternity things she'd bought were too tight now. So, while she was home, the least he could do was to help paint the nursery. He did the fussy trim and let her shove the roller around. He made the bizarre sandwiches she craved for lunch then rubbed her swollen feet before she trudged down the back stairs to go to work.

With all the brainwork done, it was time to tip off the season. It was only fitting that Flint should play its inaugural contest against the *Gunners* from Grand Rapids. Hector hoped he would be able to remain impartial. He was certain that the teams would become cross-state arch-rivals.

He lifted a fat, six-subject notebook from the briefcase. It was left over from his last semester at Port Huron College. He ripped out the notes from Modern Ideologies class. There should be enough sheets for the season though he hadn't decided how many games to play. No playoff format had been established yet, either, but those were all minor details. He found the Flint and Grand Rapids rosters then printed the starters on the first page; home team on the left, visitors on the right. Forwards were listed first. The center was on the third line, then the two guards, just like a regular box score in the newspaper. He heard a young soprano from Flint Central, maybe, or Holy Redeemer, straining through the anthem. The players had all been advised against black power salutes or other political gestures during this ceremony, at least until the team had earned some acceptance. He heard a PA announcer introducing the starters. Or was it a radio play-by-play guy? Would radio coverage hurt home attendance or promote interest?

Ballenger Field House, on the campus of the community college, was only about half full. You could blame that on the GM strike, but it was also a school night. The *LeSabres* would have to play in the old building until they could work out a deal to share Industrial Auditorium with the minor league hockey team. But that was *another* petty difficulty which wouldn't discourage a committed ownership.

Hector held six dice in his left hand including a red one. A pencil waited in his right. Each player would roll the six dice, or shots, per period. A two-spot was a basket and each single spot a free throw. Anyone who scored with the one red die could roll it again for as long as it kept scoring. A three-spot on the red die would count because Hector had adopted the new long-range-shot rule from the A.B.A. Guys who kept the red die going could really *light it up*. They would have a *hot hand*. Players who were cold, who didn't score, might have to share their playing time, meaning dice, with a substitute. They might have to sit down altogether if that guy off the bench did well.

Hector heard the ref's whistle and cheers of the curious new fans, before he dumped the dice onto the carpet.

The Flint power forward, Roland, managed a single hoop while Thompkins, the Grand Rapids player guarding him, canned two, including a red deuce. Thompkins hit a free throw with the bonus roll. Mauvier sank a basket for the *LeSabres*, but the Grand Rapids small forward Cruscewicz (Hector wasn't sure of the pronunciation) countered with two of his own from the right-side baseline:

"He hangs fire. Yeah, he drained that jumper!"

Carter, the Flint big man in the middle, chipped in a bucket -- a put-back in the paint. "He sticks home the bunny with a thunderous, two-handed slam!"

But then Brown rolled in three free throws. Even though Brown failed to convert the red one, it was clear that Carter would be in foul trouble for the next quarter. Jones, the Flint point guard drove the lane and scored a nifty reverse lay-up then added a free-throw: "A little shake-and-bake! He takes it to the hole and gets hammered!"

Brennaman then put up a pair of hoops for the *Gunners*. Gulliver, the *LeSabres'* shooting guard would have to get untracked from outside. Sure enough, he bombed a three-pointer. "From down town…bang! Nothing but bottom!" He added a free-throw with his second roll but that was it. When Suggs put up a pair from outside plus a free-throw, it left Flint down 21-13 at the end of the first quarter.

Hector cursed under his breath. The score was way too low for pro ball. He was going to end up with a college score. Should he add another dice? Yeah, but how many teams take 35 shots in a quarter? 30 shots was already unrealistic. He stood up, stretched and groped his way into the kitchen. The scarred linoleum felt grubby beneath his bare feet, but light from a security lamp in the alley made a path for him. They'd only lived in the place about six weeks, but he placed his hand precisely on the handle of the clunky, *furnished* refrigerator. It had a primitive, louvered cooling element on top. He put the gearshift-like handle in reverse. The door fell open on beer, diet colas, lunch meat, and unclaimed take-outs from the restaurant. A bulb was burned out in there too, but he found a can of *Buckeye Ale*, the A&P Store brand. The discount brew was a sacrifice he'd resigned himself to until he could get back to work. He lifted the pop-top to a cold, satisfying spurt.

So, suppose his league played a college style game with shorter quarters and zone defenses allowed? That would account for lower scores. Some fans liked defensive hoops. Yeah, but they could see college or high school ball nearby, and for a lower ticket price. *His* fans would probably demand the run-and-gun, high-scoring pro game.

Hector sat back down to the notebook, rosters, and dice. They were just dice, he reminded himself. Unless he wanted to complicate matters with some sort of handicapping system, all his players would eventually appear to be of equal talent. Those were the laws of probability and statistics. As he studied the box score further, he realized what was out of whack. Starters playing the entire first quarter without substitution was also unrealistic. Carter, especially, would have to come out before committing another foul. The *Gunners* would certainly go to work on him. Suppose he added two guys off the bench and they each rolled one die, a total of eight more shots for each team per game? O.K., and one of those dice should be the red one. It seemed like a good compromise. But when the subs on both sides came up empty, the score remained low. Hector cursed again. If there was to be a radio broadcast, this would be the time for a commercial break. Probably a beer commercial. He tipped back a swallow of the *Buckeye*. He wouldn't be writing any ad copy for *this* swill, that was certain. He went on with the second quarter.

Scoring picked up somewhat. Roland scored his second hoop with three dice and Margriff stuck home a pair with the remaining three as Roland sat down. And then Andrews played well in Carter's place, adding two field goals and a free-throw: "This young man has come off the bench smoking!"

The big story, however, was Suggs of Grand Rapids. The *Gunners* shooting guard nailed a pair inside the ark, plus a 3-pointer that he converted with a second bomb--10 points in the quarter and 15 for the half. "Someone will have to step out and put a hand in *this* guy's face!"

Flint was outscored 27-24 for the segment and had fallen behind 48-37 at half-time. If shooting continued at this pace, the final score wouldn't be too far off. Hector tinkered with the game rules some more as he took his empty to the kitchen. Yes, he would allow zone defenses but leave the game at professional length. Life was full of compromises, as he was learning. Why shouldn't sports management be any different?

He opened another *Buckeye* in the shadowy kitchen. Again, he enjoyed the cold, cracking noise, like the stresses of a frozen pond. His broadcasts would definitely have beer commercials, and there should be a car dealer. Car dealers, especially Buick, would want to advertise with the *LeSabres*. He'd need a jingle--something produced locally, with an R&B flavor. Local talent. When he reentered the living room and glanced up, Gwen was leaning in the opposite doorway. Startled, Hector nearly fumbled the beer.

Gwen's arms were folded. Her face expressed the bleary irritation of interrupted sleep. The pregnant glow was gone. Hector thought she'd look perfect wielding a rolling pin, if she knew how to bake anything. She was wearing a purple satin nightshirt with a yellow Tweety Bird resting on the swollen cargo of her tummy. Tweety did not relieve her menacing aspect.

"What *is* all this?" she asked.

"It's just to pass the time. I couldn't sleep," Hector said. "It's a game I made up when I was a kid."

"Is *that* right? When I wanted to pass some time with an *adult* activity, you couldn't be bothered."

"I'm sorry baby. I just wasn't in the...," Hector pleaded. "Don't you think it's getting kinda cumbersome? I don't even think it's *safe* at this point."

"The doctor said it's OK until the last two weeks," Gwen said, louder. "I would have *settled* for a cuddle."

"Baby, in a few months we'll be catching up. All the stuff we like to do and in the normal positions. Anyway, you were asleep," Hector added. "Did the dice wake you up, or was it the beer opening? Hey, do you want a glass?"

Gwen continued to glare. "No. No thank you. No, I thought you were talking to someone. And you were making some kinda noise. Like a blow drier. *Ahhhhh. . .*like that. I thought you were having an asthma attack or something."

"You could *hear* that? way in *there*?"

"Oh, yeah. So, what the *hell*?" she prodded.

"It was crowd noise," Hector admitted. "For the game. I musta been doing it."

"Oh, for Chrissake," Gwen grumbled. "And, by the way. Next time you're practicing for a few *months* from now while I'm at work. . ." As she slowly unfolded her arms, the foreboding that had nagged him earlier now leaped in Hector's chest. In one hand she gripped the wadded-up satin panties that went with her Tweety shirt. "Kindly play with yourself in some other way? These were under your pillow and they're all gunky!" She dropped the underwear right in the middle of the Ballenger Field House hardwood, right where the players were warming up for the second half. She turned and stalked back down the hall. "And tell your fans to shut the hell up, some people have to work in the morning."

Hector watched the door close. At least she didn't slam it. There was *some* hope there. But *geez*, he was a prize dumb-ass. When Gwen came to bed the first time, he thought the missing underwear was a signal that he could just ignore. He hadn't made the connection with the pair he'd snuck out of her drawer that afternoon. The adolescent game wasn't embarrassing enough, but now he was a neglectful self-abuser as well. There was no recourse but to make it up to her somehow--maybe fix a real sit-down dinner in the carbon encrusted oven. He should make more of an effort in the sack too; invest in a *Playboy* or something. Load up on wheat germ. But could he even trust himself to hide a *Playboy*?

For the time being though, he might as well finish the game. He just wasn't *feeling it,* as they say, to follow her back to bed. He hoped Suggs wasn't still *feeling it* for Grand Rapids in the third quarter, or the *LeSabres* could forget about rallying. And then he should probably play the late game from out west so he wouldn't get behind. He was pretty much obligated after the Des Moines *Prairies Dawgs* had made their long bus ride to face the Duluth *Lakers*.

Double Fault

Hector Fritch might have simply punched in late. On a Friday evening, the absenteeism at Fisher Body-Pontiac was usually so high that his foreman would have kissed him. He'd been indecisive all the way down Route 24 because the late September day seemed like summer. Probably the last of summer.

He'd picked up Route 24 after driving west from Celeryville, the air and light so warm and silken that he held the Comet GT well below the speed limit. A mile south on 24, he wheeled into *Mirror Lake Grocery*. He intended to eat a snack, have a beer on the way down, maybe give some thought to missing this particular night shift altogether.

He didn't have the heart to put spurs to the 302 engine as he slipped back into traffic. A *Schlitz Tall Boy* rode between his legs in a slender bag. A red-hot sausage and a pickled egg sat in a cardboard tray on the other bucket seat. The first of three pretzel sticks was clenched in the corner of his mouth like a stogie. When he realized that he'd left his coffee thermos at home, it seemed like an omen.

Going into *LeRoy's Bar* was another critical hesitation. *LeRoy's* was located on Baldwin Avenue just across from Employee Gate 2. Ten acres of parking lot stretched behind it. Night shift cars baked and pinged as evening fell. Both entrances to *LeRoy's* were propped open. A floor fan in the corner behind the pool table thrummed softly. A small oscillating fan on the end of the bar also churned the dark, stale air. Above it, the television had been muted during the local news from Detroit. Wayne, one of the bartenders, worked on the kitchenette side. He pulled a chain to turn on a fluorescent light. Fritch soon smelled browning meat as Wayne started the sauce for Coney dogs. This began to displace the accumulated funk of stale beer, tobacco, and body odor.

There were only three customers in the place--two guys he didn't recognize, nearly sprawled over the bar but still slurring back and forth. Probably from day shift. Then he saw Curtis Baffle from the door glass sub-assembly operation just up the line. Curtis studied the juke box. LeRoy Petty sat further back, reading something on the desk in his little office.. His girth didn't quite fit the swivel chair which creaked in protest as he readjusted his buttocks. A stack of longneck cases decorated the back wall.

"Fritch! Ya'll comin' or goin'?" Curtis turned, cupping a fistful of quarters that he hadn't fed into the juke yet. Conway Twitty *bomp, bomp, bomm'd* behind him.

"Haven't decided," Hector said, lifting himself onto a stool. "Let's see how I feel."

"It's like cookout weather. Bet they hadda shut down for relief."

"Wouldn't wanta spoil *that*, would I? On the other hand, I don't wanta end up with them paying me on Fridays." He waited for Wayne to notice him.

"Ya'll don't hardly miss no time no ways," Curtis said. "Me, I already got a verbal warning. Ya'll decide to go in, you never seen me, OK?"

"Goes without saying." Hector could not fathom why Curtis didn't simply go in, build up his door-glass then skip out at lunch. Those guys worked their asses off for four hours, then clocked each other out at the end of the shift. Maybe the first part was too hard for Curtis on a warm day, or maybe it wasn't his turn to leave early.

The bartender bounced down to Fritch's end, wiping his hands with a linen service rag. "What'll it be?"

Hector hesitated. A quick shell or a longneck of *Strohs* and some more food to start soaking it up? "Are you gonna have the Tiger game on?"

"I dunno. They ain't catchin' the Orioles," Wayne said. "Ain't you got any money on the old guy and that woman libber? Big tennis match."

"Oh! I *forgot* that was tonight. Billie Jean King and Bobby Riggs."

"That ol' boy sounds like he's about half a queer his own self," called Curtis.

"Anyways. I think LeRoy wants to watch him whup her ass."

"Well, *damn*. O.K. Guess I'll have a *Strohs* and...how about a bag of that cheese popcorn?" Fritch sighed, his mind clawing for rationalizations. The house payment had been made for the month. Check. They were starting to get some overtime as the '74 models were introduced. Check. Car insurance, though, next week. Three hours overtime already, versus missing eight hours straight time tonight. Would they dare work nine hours if they had to shut down for relief? Quality would be lousy. But if they really needed the cars? He had to think management wouldn't hesitate. They'd bring people in tomorrow or even Sunday to make repairs. But something was lurking, something he'd forgotten. When was the house insurance due again?

Wayne brought the beer. Fritch opened his bag of popcorn. George Jones finished groaning out of the speakers about some guy who died and finally quit pining over an old girlfriend. Then, (why should he be surprised), "Born to be Wild" started up. Curtis Baffle, without the support of the big Wurlitzer juke, weaved toward an empty stool. "Well, shit! It *feels* like summer, don't it?"

Fritch smiled and nodded. Summer, fall, they had begun to run in together for him. He earned six credit hours in one summer session at University of Michigan-Flint Campus, then three in the next. He took Gwen on exactly *one* long weekend to Traverse City, just before the end of the model-change break. That was their summer vacation unless you counted the two weeks Wesley spent at his grandparents farm down by Litchfield.

They went to a dinky zoo in Traverse City and then to a play at Cherry County Playhouse. Buddy Ebsen and his daughter starred in *Our Town,* then came out to tap-dance for the curtain call. It was bizarre watching Jed Clampett hoofing around on the stage. Then Gwen couldn't *quite* have an orgasm so she got pissed off at *him.* He cracked another beer out of the cooler while she wept. She shed more tears at the motel than she did when the Ebsen girl's character died in childbirth. Wesley came home spoiled, and was just now getting squared back around to bearable.

Maybe that's what was bothering him. It was either that Wesley needed a chunk of cash to start nursery school or that his own tuition refund might be ready at the front office. Just as well he hadn't gone in and picked it up. He might have walked right back over here with it.

"What channel's that supposed t' be on? " Wayne dragged a step-stool under the television.

"ABC's promotin' it. Channel 7," LeRoy called. He stepped out of the office and closed the door, carrying a white *Koegel Meats* box under his arm.

That would be the foot-long franks for lunch rush. "They'll be playin' just about the time Trim Shop lunch comes in. Don't go puttin' on the dog-ass Tigers. I don't care what nobody says. The customer ain't always right when I've made a wager."

Fritch could see the snub-nosed handgun on LeRoy's straining belt as he lifted the counter bridge and entered the kitchenette.

"I hear ya, boss," Wayne said. "You know anything about tennis?" he asked Fritch.

"Enough to knock it back and forth. I'm O.K. up 'til forty. I get confused when it gets to tie breakers, who's advantage it is and all that."

"Ya'll got to win by two, though, right?" Curtis rested his chin in the palms of his hands, watching the channels go by until Wayne stopped on Channel 7. Sergeant Carter shouted right in the face of Gomer Pyle, so the rerun after the news was showing. It wouldn't be long before the preliminary jawing for the big *Battle of the Sexes* began. "Like in ping-pong?"

"Jesus H. Christ," LeRoy muttered. Already, steam had begun to roll up from the footlongs in a broad, stainless steel pan. This was placed in a counter-top space next to the meat sauce. LeRoy squatted with some difficulty to fiddle with the gas burners underneath. Then he switched on the yellow warming lamps above the service counter. "They'll *explain* it to you hillbillies on the broadcast. Don't hardly anybody watchin'll know anything 'cept it's an old hustler and that uppity bitch. They're playin' for $100 grand, winner take all. What more d'ya need to know?"

"Well, I was just astin'," Curtis whined.

Wayne winked at Fritch. "Would you believe ol' LeRoy been divorced three times."

"Only three?" Fritch had nothing against women's rights or liberation. But then, he'd been exposed at school to the principles behind it. He was younger, anyway, and from a different cultural background than many of the auto workers. He had never wished to be in charge of anyone in the first place. Least of all women, of whom, he understood, he was sometimes too much in awe. Freedom was freedom, right? And shoprats were forever going on about their rights and freedoms. What was good for the goose should be...well, he *thought* he believed that. Plus, look at the benefits: Feathered hair, skirts any length they wanted. Or, those tight jeans that showed off navels and pelvic bones. Hey, would anybody be *braless* without the Movement? They forgot about *that.* Even Gwen left hers off and went bobbling around when she didn't have to work. Women in bars were asking men to dance. He'd *seen* it.

"Yeah, he got burned a couple times, for *certain.* Last one got a piece of the bar." Wayne began to set up shot glasses and other pre-ordered drinks for the lunch rush. "He can't say no longer, *he's a lover, not a fighter.*"

Fritch did his best to pace himself. After a second *Strohs,* he tried a glass of club soda. He didn't need to get stupid and end up with a drunk driving bust. No more days off if *that* happened. There were back roads he could navigate going home, but they weren't entirely risk free. He'd been followed before, observed by the law. He'd driven well enough for long enough while crapping in his shorts, more-or-less figuratively. His route into Lapeer County would track along narrow gravel back-roads where glare-eyed possums and coons looked him over with the same skepticism. Or, he could still go in to work after lunch and plead car trouble. He knew *someone* would see him in *LeRoy's* at lunch. Luckily, his foreman was a regular at *Ventura Lounge* down the street. Fritch could also just go on home. Send the babysitter home early and save Gwen a few bucks.

On the screen, preliminary buffoonery had commenced in the Astrodome. Riggs entered in a rickshaw drawn by a team of well-endowed models. Billie Jean played along, riding into the arena on a Cleopatra-throne litter held aloft by four bronzed pretty-boys.

"Turn it up!" LeRoy yelled.

Wayne put the bag of footlong buns down and climbed up to reach the volume. It was already twenty after eight. Deanne and Toni, the lunch-rush barmaids, were just putting on their black change-aprons. Toni took over laying buns into a steamer. A row of paper sleeves for the foot-longs waited on the top of the serving counter.

"She ain't even pretty," she said, cracking her chewing gum.

"I wouldn't sleep with *either* of 'em," Deanne sneered.

Now the two adversaries exchanged gag gifts. Billie Jean delivered a struggling piglet into her opponent's embrace. Then Riggs gave her a giant *Slo-Poke* sucker. Fritch understood the symbolism of the pig. But, could the guy *possibly* be that obtuse? The sexual suggestion would be as far as *LeRoy's* customers would take it but it had to mean something else. Well, but he *was* a hustler and she was supposedly the mark. That *had* to be what he was getting at.

"She got some legs on her, though, huh?" Curtis mumbled. Merle Haggard was challenging someone's patriotism, still on Curtis's money, when LeRoy shut off the jukebox.

"She's a big gal," Fritch agreed. He didn't bother wasting adjectives like *lithe* or *feline*, though he was reassured of his sobriety level that he'd thought of them.

A few workers had straggled in as Body Shop lunch began. Those guys had to walk from way in the back of the plant. Pretty soon, as the first volleys were hit between Riggs and King, the Trim Shop horn blared across the street. The sound, with many of the plant's windows opened, tugged momentarily at Fritch's conscience. Then the hoard came thundering out the gate as uniformed Plant Security stepped aside. The assault on the Coneys and alcohol was broken only by traffic on Baldwin and the crosswalk signal.

Drinkers tended to pile in the front door, shouting their orders or snatching drinks that were already set up and paid for. Eaters lined up from the kitchenette out the back door and onto the sidewalk. The girls took their money while working between tables to bring out orders. LeRoy tonged out another armload of footlongs and added sauce. He lifted a basket of onion rings out of the deep-fryer. After a forkful of minced onion, each customer added the condiment of choice--usually hot sauce or cayenne pepper seeds. Some left immediately, back against the flow. Others stood against the wall, trying not to block the view of drinkers who hogged the tables.

"Oh c'mon, you ol' bastard! Stay back!"

"She runnin' him all over."

"He ain't got the legs no more!"

"An' that ain't all if he's anything like *my* old man!" A lady worker cackled.

"There! She idn't gettin' t' that soft junk hit behind her! That's what he's gotta do!"

"It's called a lob, dip-shit! Can't you *hear* the man?" another lady shouted.

"Christ! Ten more minutes, I gotta run!"

"She ain't *playin'* his game's what they're sayin'. She's layin' back."

"'Bout all they're *good* for though idn't it?"

"That old *man* ain't no fair test."

As abruptly as the lunch rush began, the shoprats stood, draining their longnecks and drafts. Hard-core individuals at the bar on both sides of Fritch knocked back shots of whiskey before heading to the door. Most took their foot-longs with them.

"Fritch! Hey, I didn't see *you* when I come in!" Marty Boulanger reached over Hector's shoulder to place an empty bottle on the bar. Marty installed tail-light moldings in an adjacent work group. They sometimes car-pooled from Celeryville when Fritch wasn't taking classes. "You was smart to skip. It's too damn nice out. Why don't you do me a favor and call me out? We're gonna be in there past last call."

Fritch turned on the vinyl stool cushion. "You *sure*? What's my story?"

"Uh, shit. You ain't never gonna sound like my wife and *she* sure won't call me out," Boulanger said. "O.K., how's this? You're my brother-in-law Melvin, because Susan had to take Jr. to Emergency. It's, it's...lemme think. O.K., make it just, like, an allergic reaction or something. Uh...like a hornet sting."

"Is there anybody even *in* South Trim Office to answer the phone?"

Boulanger frowned. "They're so thin they got a couple of foremen on the line. We're writing a shit-load of grievances. Just give it a shot. Let it ring. If it don't work out, well, ain't nothing lost."

"I can try."

"If I get clear, I'll buy a round. Just stay here."

"They'd have to cover you pretty quick. I'm gonna pull out when *this* is over." Fritch hiked his thumb at the television where Riggs was mopping his brow as the players switched sides.

"Well, thanks anyway. I'll owe ya one."

"O.K. Just let me see if I've got this: Junior's sick. Allergic reaction. I'm Melvin, your brother-in-law, calling for your wife because she's gone to Emergency. In Lapeer?"

"There ya go. I better haul ass!"

When the patrons from South Trim had gone back to work, Fritch remained, now fully committed to his stool and a night of truancy. He ordered another *Strohs*, his fourth at *LeRoys*, he believed, though well spaced. He'd been in the place nearly four hours. Then he remembered the *Tall Boy* guzzled on the way down. But he was still steady on his feet when he went to the men's room.

There were a few additional bodies gaping at the tennis spectacle--sub-assembly workers who had built up enough door glass or other components to let them to skip out. Riggs, forced by King's strategy to come to the net, had lost the first set, 6-4. The old hustler increased his clowning. He clutched at straws to delay the inevitable, calling time-out for an injury. A trainer animatedly massaged his wrist.

"Stick a fork in 'im," Curtis Baffle mumbled, before swallowing his last bite of Coney. Head unsteady, on a neck in need of shaving, he wiped his mouth on the sleeve of his work shirt. "He's done."

Fritch tipped the *Strohs* for short sips. He dug the number for South Trim Office out of his wallet. He waited for Toni to get off the pay phone on the wall between the restroom doors.

As he suspected, the South Trim phone rang and rang. He knew that a loud buzzer above the door should alert foremen on the shop floor. Someone must answer it eventually--the General Foreman would finish putting out a fire somewhere or a line foreman could dash in and take the call when he had a chance. Finally, a voice, short of breath, responded. "Yeah, what!?"

"This South Trim Office? This where Marty Boulanger works?"

"This is where a whole bunch a dumb sums-a-bitches works!"

"Who am I speaking to?"

"Who'm *I* speaking to? You sound *familiar*. This is Arnie Forfahr, Assistant General Foreman. Except tonight I'm working repair. Even our clerk ain't here!"

Fritch knew Forfahr from when Arnie was foreman of the water-test inspectors. Fritch sometimes hung shields on the front of the car bodies before they entered the spray booth. The inspectors, armed with clipboards and black-lights, boarded the cars halfway through to check for leaks. Forfahr was the foreman to gripe at when the shields didn't come back fast enough on the monorail.

"*Oh*. Well, I need to get a message to Marty Boulanger. You don't know where he works?"

"Yeah, I heard of him. All I can do is look him up and notify his boss. I don't have time to chase him down in person."

"That's fine. His kid got a hornet sting and swelled all up, tell him. I'm Marty's brother-in-law. My sister had to drive the kid to Emergency in Lapeer."

"Wow," Forfahr chuckled. "That's a pretty *good* one. *That* one took some thought. You sure I don't *know* you?"

"Listen, it's the real deal. Something bad happens and Marty wasn't told..."

"Yeah? You some kinda shop lawyer, too? Spare me. I'll get in touch with your...*brother-in-law* when I get time. No way in hell are we getting him out of here, though."

"All we're asking is that he's notified, sir."

"And maybe I'll give Lapeer Regional a call." Forfahr chuckled and hung up.

Fritch peed again before returning to his stool. Riggs had lost the second set, 6-3. Winded and perspiring heavily, he'd been forced to a precarious 5-3 score in the set that could end his evening. He managed to hold serve after first double faulting, but was soon forced to deuce. Wayne tried to wake Curtis Baffle.

"C'mon now, I'm gonna have to 86 yer ass, you can't stay in a upright position."

"Jus' restin' my eyes. Ain't this over yet?"

"Yer just in time."

Fritch agonized whether or not to have one more for the road. He compromised by ordering a draft. Wayne brought it as Riggs returned service of match point into the net. Billie Jean flung her racket toward the Astrodome roof. Riggs, clearly played out, managed gamely to jump the net to congratulate her. The neon buzz of beer logos behind the bar, the hum of the coolers, and the soft pulse of the fan were drowned out by the cheering throng around the two athletes on television. The scraping of LeRoy's steel spatula moving used grease off the grill continued unabated.

"I underestimated you," Riggs told King. The words seemed to hang in the warm bar where none of the drinkers could mistake them.

"Well, ain't that the shits," Curtis said.

After finishing the draft and settling his tab, Fritch stepped into the sultry night air. The beginning sliver of a harvest moon had climbed high enough to be seen beyond the edifice of the plant. He strolled in the opposite direction, happy to be parked in the back of the Fisher Body lot. It gave him time for a walk and deep breaths.

He looked at his watch in the light of a security lamp. There was plenty of time to sit in the Comet before the night shift came out; maybe listen to the radio awhile just to make sure he was O.K. for the road. He wasn't going to get home before Gwen now, anyway. But it probably wouldn't be a good idea to fall asleep. He turned the ignition key. He would get home too early, his clothes reeking of cigarette smoke, to have worked a full shift; but not so late that he might have been out trolling. Short pay, no help with the babysitter, and he'd probably dropped $20. He could only hope that Gwen had a good night of tips, and that she'd buy into his excuses. The weather in Celeryville would have been just as fine. And if she'd seen the tennis match that the cooks at *Titus Family Restaurant* had surely watched, well… Just maybe there'd be some of that joy for the underdog left over for him.

Water Test

A t the end of the last night shift before Thanksgiving in 1975, Hector Fritch worked up the assembly-line so he could be first in line at the time clock. His job was carrying water-test shields and attaching them to the fronts of car bodies so that windshields and other glass could be inspected for leaks. At that point in the process, there was no engine, hood or front fenders on the car. Fritch had to stand on the front of the dolly to snap both attachments because his partner on the passenger side was stuck near the spray booth with other duties.

Fritch caught his breath after the exertion. The molded fiberglass and foam-rubber shields with the steel carry-bar weighed nearly forty pounds. The line moved forward at a rate of fifty-seven cars per hour. He had to hang a shield then run for another one as they came dripping on a conveyor from the end of the booth. His clothes were always damp from the shields and humidity from the booth. Now he'd worked up a sweat, too. He hoped management wouldn't suddenly decide to work a few cars worth of overtime. Pretty soon, a boisterous mob of Fisher Body workers fell in behind him to wait for the horn. Some carried empty casserole dishes after impromptu work-group feasts. More than a few had been drinking, getting another kind of head start on the four day weekend. Gwen should have the station wagon waiting across the street in the parking lot of *Ventura Lounge*.

Fritch had caught a ride down to work with another shop-rat from Celeryville named Marty Boulanger. Marty owed him one. That way, Gwen could work her shift at *Titus Family Restaurant*, pack up the car and the kid and meet him at the end of *his* shift. Gwen's parents had recently found work on a big dairy farm down by Litchfield. A modest farm house near the operation came with the deal. Gwen's father, whose official title was *herdsman*, had to supervise the milking of two hundred head through the holidays. It was just easier, Fritch believed, for Gwen to meet him at the plant. They could get the three-hour drive over with and then sleep in. Even though this was just their second trip down there and in the dead of night, it beat sleeping for a few hours at home then hitting the road early. It was also fifty miles closer this way.

Hector rang his time-card when the shift klaxon sounded. Sprinting feet splashed around him as he dashed out the gate. A cold drizzle was falling. Plenty of workers headed straight into *Ventura Lounge* for last call. Others made it to the company parking-lot. Impatient traffic escaped in three directions. Amber parking lamps gleamed where other spouses waited in the bar's parking-lot.

"Shhh. Don't slam," Gwen whispered as Fritch clambered in on the driver's side. "He's been fired up all evening and he finally crashed." Wesley, their four-year-old, sprawled, mouth open, in the backseat. His nest was fashioned with pillows, a quilt, and the remains of a McDonalds take-out. Gwen reached over the seat to salvage a half-empty orange drink and a few surviving French fries.

"Any trouble finding the place?" Fritch put the big Mercury in gear. He eased over the low curb and into the street. Someone in the line of departing cars let him in while giving him the finger.

"Besides that it faces on two different streets and has four employee gates? No. There sure are a lot of bars. You guys could get in trouble."

"Some do."

"And *this* dive could use a bigger sign. A guy came out questioning everybody. He had a clipboard."

"That woulda been Arnie, the owner," Fritch said. "He was my first committee- man when I hired in. He took a *piece-of-the-rock*, as they used to say. Made sweetheart deals on a bunch of grievances during the last contract talks. Then he mysteriously retired. I'm a lunch regular and it was just for tonight."

"Yeah. I told him our name and he moved on."

Fritch worked their way through the city streets and stoplights until they reached Route 59. They had to head west to get to U.S. 23. Bars along the way appeared to be very busy near closing time. "College kids are home for Thanksgiving," he said wistfully.

"Awww, sweetie. I'm *so* sorry," Gwen cooed. "You get to go at Company expense. And you have a *home*, too."

"Yeah, and I wish we were going there right now."

Gwen frowned in the dashboard lights. "Oh bullshit, babe. When you get started drinking with Stan and Delbert, *I'll* feel like the outsider."

Stan and Delbert were Gwen's younger brothers. They still lived with her parents and had been taken on at the dairy farm. Delbert was signed up to leave soon for basic training in the Navy.

"Yeah, yeah. I'll try not to ignore you. But *they're* usually buying. And your Mom'll put about ten pounds on me."

"Well, you could always just push your plate away after three helpings. No one holds a gun to your head." Gwen lifted a thermos off the floor and poured the cap half full of steaming coffee. She guided it into Fritch's hand.

The traffic on Route 59 thinned out by the time they turned south. He planned to pick up the Interstate near Ann Arbor which headed west. Gwen kept the FM radio playing with the volume down. She rolled the window down a crack and blew smoke toward it. "Tell me when you need me to drive."

"I'm pretty wired for now. Anyway, I wake right up when *you* drive. Sorry."

"Fine."

They listened to music and the soft, condescending voice of the disc jockey until they'd made it nearly to Jackson. Middle-of-the-night truck traffic between Detroit and Chicago was swelled by families going *over the river and through the woods*. Fritch wondered how many others in this parade were traveling after a night shift somewhere. Driving rain didn't seem to slow anyone much. He turned the wiper interval up all the way, grateful that this wasn't snow.

"Dude wants us to know he's hip and we're not."

"He talks so *low*. He's making me sleepy," Gwen said.

After Fritch found the exit to head south for Litchfield, Gwen put the map back into the glove compartment. She wedged her head into a pillow against the door. The secondary roads were nearly deserted. They passed the intersection leading to Albion. There was a small, private college there. Fritch doubted if any shop-rats used their tuition assistance at Albion. "Oh, hey," he looked over to see if Gwen was still awake. "Did that old guy come in tonight or did he go home?"

Gwen sighed. "Who? Paul Steadman? He's not *that* old. He's just lonely in that crummy motel. And yeah, I think he said he was driving to Indiana somewhere. He didn't order dinner, just coffee to go."

"What does he do again?"

"Some kind of geological survey. They're looking for gas and oil deposits. He's got two other guys under him."

"He's trying to get *you* under him," Fritch chuckled. "I've seen those crews parked along the roads ever since the Oil Embargo. They string out wires and probes then send sound waves into the ground."

Gwen was silent. She played with the radio trying to find something besides country that would come in clearly.

"What? Did I touch a nerve? Did he finally ask you out?"

"You *wish*. But I'm still not screwing anybody for *your* entertainment. We've been over that."

"Was that a *yes*?"

"It's not a big deal. It was like, just a general invitation. Robin and Dianne and I were already talking about going out to *Celeryville Lanes* for a drink next Friday after work. He just sort of threw in that we should let him know and he'd meet us to buy us a drink. He's just lonely."

"Well, of *course* he is. With a middle-aged wife three hundred miles away? And a friendly waitress twenty years younger? You can go have a drink with him if you want."

"I'm *aware* of that. But it'll be if *I* want."

"Right. Of course. But please explain to me how you'd go about screwing someone for *my* entertainment if I wasn't even there?"

"I think you like to play with it in your head. You wanta hear everything I ever did with anyone. For your precious mental *images*. Say, I think there's something wrong with this radio."

"We're just out of range."

"No, babe. It's getting dim. I can't get any volume from anywhere."

Just as Fritch looked down at the radio dial, the alternator light came on in front of him. "Awww, crap! Quick, just turn it off!" Their hands touched as he reached down to turn off the defroster and blower. On the steering column, he cut the wipers back to the slowest setting. "Crack your window so we don't fog up."

"What's going on?"

"Damned alternator must be going bad." Fritch turned a knob to kill the dashboard lights altogether. He tapped the headlight switch from high beams to dim. Their visibility wasn't *too* bad. The rain had slackened. "How much farther do we have to go?"

"Eight or ten miles, I think. Maybe. We went through that wide spot called Homer. I'll need the dome light if you want me to look at the map. Shouldn't we find a phone or something?"

"Well, if we *see* one. But, look around. I don't think there are any more towns."

Fritch slowed after another mile as the headlights began to fail. Suddenly, a glimmer of other headlights flashed in the rearview mirror. He tried to gauge the closing rate of the other car and wondered how well his own taillights could be seen. He hoped that the other motorist wasn't one of those homecoming students roaring back to mom and dad's house with a good buzz going.

The car behind them slowed as it caught up. Probably checking them out, maybe recognizing their predicament, Fritch thought. If it was a cop, that might not be the worst thing. Cautiously, the trailing vehicle moved into the other lane to pass. "Hang on. Let's see if we can use this guy for a while."

The driver honked as he completed the pass. Fritch tromped on the accelerator, attempting to keep pace. The station wagon bogged down, missing, as the timing chain lost its count. The car coughed and lurched, but kept going. Luckily, the overtaking driver did not hurtle away but seemed to slow down to accommodate them. Fritch tried to close up behind without making the situation any more dangerous. His own headlights were now two weak spots on the trunk of the lead car.

"I think we caught a break," Fritch said, after a few miles of studying the guy's rear bumper and the dividing lines on the black-top. The Mercury sounded like it was running on about five of its eight cylinders. "Plus this battery isn't very old."

"O.K., see that water tower up there? See the lights?" Gwen hunched forward. "We have to make a left just before we get into Litchfield. Or, we can go on into town. There might be a phone booth."

"But they're what? A mile out of town? I think we can make it."

He could see a village limits sign as they stopped at a crossroads. The motor chugged precariously but kept running. The Samaritan who'd led them made his stop, honked again then crept toward town. Fritch tried to honk back but his own horn bleated like a sick lamb. He muscled through the left turn, the power steering nearly gone.

Now on gravel, each washboard ripple sent thudding geysers of water and mud against the floor-pan of the car.

"Can you see *anything?*" Fritch asked.

"I could see the shoulder, the ditch or whatever if I could run this window down."

"Never mind. We don't have enough juice to get it back up. I *think* we're in the middle of the road. My night vision's kicking in."

"Looks like they've left the porch light on," Gwen said as the engine died.

Fritch used the last of the wagon's momentum to get out of the way, rolling as far toward the shoulder as he dared. "If that's *their* porch light." Unfamiliar as he was with his in-law's new home, he could not recall any deep ditches. They came to a stop as the car began to tilt ever so slightly on the passenger side. "So near, and yet so far."

They sat in silence for a few moments. Random drops of rain pinged on the roof. These might be falling from a tree for all Fritch knew. At least it wasn't the earlier drumming torrent. Fritch tried to see out Gwen's window but it was beaded and opaque with the vapor of their breathing. The temperature must be dropping, Fritch thought. "Well, it sure coulda been worse."

"How? We won't find anybody to fix this before Friday or Saturday. I doubt if Dad can even *tow* it until after dinner, with all those cows to do."

"Well, but maybe he knows somebody. Del and Stan have kept shitty cars running for as long as I've known them."

"I guess that's their calling, " Gwen said flatly. She unbuckled her seat belt. She raised up to peer back at Wesley.

"I *meant* that we drove a long way, practically blind, through a storm that wasn't snow. Luckily. And now we've got just a short walk. Maybe a quarter-mile, looks like." Fritch unbuckled his own belt. He wriggled into the denim work coat that he'd draped over the seat. It smelled of raw plastics and lubricants. "I'll hump down there and wake somebody up. We'll come right back for you."

"Like *hell*," Gwen said, no longer whispering. "We could get rammed in the dark. *We're* not staying here alone."

"Oh, c'mon. It's gotta be four-thirty in the morning. You're gonna get soaked and muddy. Wes is gonna get wet. Don't you want your clothes and stuff down at the house?"

"I don't care. Figure something out. We're not waiting here."

Fritch shook his head at this tipping point of frustration. He thumped down hard on the steering wheel with both hands. Of *course*, she wouldn't let him keep this simple. The windshield was now completely steamed up. All he could see through it was a glimmer of the distant porch light and a yard light he remembered at the corner of the barn. "See if there's a rain poncho in a little pouch under the seat."

Gwen groped under her side of the seat.

"There should be a flashlight and a dinky umbrella, too, next to the spare tire," he continued. "I can't vouch for the batteries but all I have to do is set every damn suitcase, shoe, and toy out on the ground to get at it."

Gwen held the poncho packet over in front of Fritch's nose. "So? *Do* it. I'll wear *this* and I can carry two suitcases."

"Better wake Wes up, then. If I'm carrying *him*, maybe *he* can carry the umbrella."

"See? There you go. Problem solving *and* a family adventure."

"Swell. *This* you want for an adventure?" Fritch sighed. "I'll need my toilet kit with my inhaler."

He swung out, testing the road's surface. His first step raised a splash. The second was merely a sloppy crunch. There seemed to be no standing water at the immediate rear of the station wagon. The luggage would be alright there. He scratched around in the dark until the key slipped into the latch. When he raised the tailgate, Wes was leaning into the cargo space.

"We broke down," the boy giggled.

"Well, I'm glad *you're* having fun. Maybe you can carry *me*."

"Uh-uh. I'm not awake."

Fritch picked out the things they'd want in the morning. He placed pairs of shoes and a few toys on top of the luggage then raised the lid on the tool space. Gwen climbed out after helping Wesley into his shoes and coat. The clear poncho had a hood. She spread her arms. "Check it out; I'm the angel of storms." The poncho covered her suitcase in one hand plus the shaving kit and Wes's duffel bag in the other. She tried to spread her arms.

"Sure." Fritch tested the flashlight in her direction. The beam seemed strong enough. He popped the umbrella, wrapped the boy's fists around the handle then lifted him easily onto his shoulders. That water-test job might have some conditioning benefits to make up for being wet all the time.

Gwen locked the doors and slammed the tailgate. The sound died in the mist. Fritch set out toward the farm lights. His flash beam played over the ruts ahead of them. "Stay close. I'll steer us around the puddles."

When they climbed the back porch steps to the kitchen door, shoes squishing, Gwen's mother had just gotten up to put the bird in the oven. No car lights had announced their arrival so she jumped at Gwen's single loud knock. She peered out and then unlocked. Wes piled into her arms, already blurting his part of the story.

Fritch might have expected shallow sleep after five years on night shift. Like a fool, he sipped even more coffee as they tried to unwind around the kitchen table. Gwen's father stumbled out to greet them before beginning his day in the milking parlor. Gwen's mother bustled around the kitchen. The adrenalin rush of a journey that had turned perilous kept them talking until, finally, words grew drowsily spaced.

The couple was favored with a spare room on the second floor while Wesley would eventually crawl into bed with his Grandma. The infidelity with which Fritch had begun to tempt Gwen flickered a reprise in his mind as they climbed the stairs. Gwen slept in panties, too tired to rummage a nightie from her things. Fritch knew she usually ditched the bra after her shift, but its absence as she undressed piqued his imagination anyway. So, the drowsing mental images should have been pleasant rather then disturbing.

With his back to the wall, he spooned up to Gwen in the small bed. He suspected that this was the twin bed of her youth, in which they had first made love with tractors and hay wagons raising dust in the nearby fields outside Celeryville. He pressed into her backside, but she was already asleep. He lacked the determination to persist. Long minutes later, three men in his dream were trying to take Wes. Fritch mumbled a warning and lunged, tackling the ring-leader. Gwen hit the floor with a scream. Fritch fell, half on top of her, his legs kicking out against the tangled sheet as he sprang.

"What!? What the *fuck*!?" she shouted.

Gasping, Fritch pushed himself up to minimize any hurt he might have inflicted. He let her loose from under him. "It's OK! It's OK!"

"Jesus Christ! Are you nuts?!"

"I...I started to have a dream." Fritch sat back up on the bed. "You better sleep on the inside."

"What was it? Football?" Gwen stood slowly. She stretched her back and flexed her knee then crawled over him. Facing the wall, she rearranged the covers.

"Some guys were taking Wes. Plus, then my leg spazzed. I'll tell you about it in the morning."

"I can't *wait*," Gwen sighed. "Try not to dream about hockey or wrestling, OK?"

Fritch recovered his share of the bedding. One foot still hung out, tapping time to the caffeine hum in his brain. He saw the face of the kidnapper as he tried to keep his eyes closed. He'd never actually *met* Paul Steadman from Indiana, but the guy *did* have two other men in his crew. "At least we're all here," Fritch mumbled.

Gwen's slow breathing had turned to a soft snore.

Muscle

In 1975, Hector Fritch didn't have enough seniority to avoid lay-off at the auto plant. Another war in the Middle East a few years before had led to steep gas prices. There was a brief panic about energy consumption. For a time, car buyers lost interest in the big Pontiacs Hector helped build. He was laid-off before Christmas again so that GM wouldn't owe him holiday pay.

Hector's wife, Gwen, kept her waitress job while Hector stayed home with their four-year-old, Wesley. Now that he was home every night, the place became a destination for several of Hector's single friends. Hector told Terry Wickersham that they would have to *cool it* after New Years because he planned to go back to college for a few classes. *"Generous" Motors* was still obligated to pay tuition assistance under the contract. The government subsidized this largess because Hector's job was being displaced by small, foreign cars. They called it a *Trade Readjustment Allowance*.

On the Friday evening before Christmas, Hector and Terry drank a special, dark Yuletide lager. Terry brought over a case of it. His father had paid him for working in their resale store, a barn packed with garage sale finds. In the afternoon, Fritch and Terry started a batch of chili with jalapenos floating in it. Terry suggested that Hector call Gwen at *Titus Family Restaurant* and remind her to invite one of her waitress friends.

"She'll get pissed off. They aren't supposed to take calls."

"What's the difference if you call or go in? They don't care when you go *in*."

"But I'm usually picking up take-out."

"C'mon, man. Maybe Robin Hebert is working."

"Gwen'll be tired. She wants to shop tomorrow after she gets her check."

"Nah. She'll wanta drink a few to unwind. She'll want some chili."

It was almost dark so Hector turned on the tree lights in the front window. He and Gwen had bought a large old home on the main residential street of Celeryville. It was run down so the price was right. They got a good interest rate and a low down-payment from Farm Home Loan Administration. Celeryville counted as a rural community.

"I'll call after I feed Wes," Hector said. "But *you've* gotta help me out tomorrow."

Wickersham leaned his bushy head over the large pot of chili. He had brought the peppers, grown and dried from his father's garden. "Just name it. I don't have to work until Sunday." He stirred with a long wooden spoon. Hector had to keep an eye on him or the chili would end up too hot for most people to eat.

"I have to go down to Pontiac. A guy owes me money and I don't wanta go alone."

Wickersham replaced the lid on the kettle. "I don't have to be your muscle, do I?" Terry was tall and his crooked nose made him look like a hockey goon. But Hector had never met a less aggressive person. As an original hippy-type in the village, Terry had to constantly walk away from harassment.

After lighting the tree, Hector spread newspapers on the floor in front of the television. He lifted Wes's little table into the center of the papers. He turned the set on. "Oh, no. You're *not* the muscle," he laughed. "But two guys might look like something. It won't be a problem. You just have to stay in the car with Wes."

"So. Who owes *you* money? *That* doesn't sound right."

"A guy from the shop. He was supposed to have it when I went down for my last check. I couldn't find him."

"Well, it sounds like he's *already* a problem. I'm telling you; I *cannot* be the muscle. I'm still on probation for that taillight out when I had a roach in the ashtray."

Hector heard Wesley padding down the hall upstairs. The boy's nap had given Hector a good break, but he'd wasted it drinking with Wickersham. He'd skipped his own nap. He reminded himself that this sloth would have to cease when he went back to school. "Come on down, buddy," he called. "I thought you already picked up trash along the road or something for that bust."

"You *know* I did. You drove by hooting on me. But I'm still on probation and I don't feel like getting *shot* down in Pontiac."

Wickersham came into the front room and admired the tree. He watched a few flurries descend through the streetlight at the corner of Frederick and Main. He took a deep pull on the longneck of murky lager.

"There's no chance of that. He's just an old hillbilly and kind of an alky."

"My friend, that's practically the *definition* of getting shot."

Hector didn't tell Wickersham that Preacher Clevinger had already burned him with a bad check. Preacher had worked on a window molding job just up the line. He always offered Hector slugs from the pint of *Jack Daniel* in his lunch box. During the final week of the second shift at Fisher Body-Pontiac, Hector sold him six Super Eight porno movies for sixty dollars. Preacher was desperate to own the films which featured the legendary John Holmes. Hector had been in a panic about the future and how to pay for Christmas. He would've sold his projector, too, if Preacher didn't already have one. It was a good deal for both because Clevinger was an older worker from Tennessee and claimed to be uncomfortable going into an adult store.

When the check bounced, Hector tracked down Clevinger's phone number. He was surprised that the address was also available from Directory Assistance. On the phone, they agreed to meet at *LeRoy's Bar* across from the plant after picking up their last paychecks. But Clevinger didn't show up. Hector was losing patience. Preacher was friendly enough when drunk on the job. But just because Hector had long hair, Preacher was always nudging him, kidding that he wanted to have sex with Hector because he looked so pretty. Sometimes Hector wondered how much of that was just goofing around.

Wesley came down the stairs slowly, still groggy. He smiled from ear to ear when he saw Wickersham.

"Hey there, little dude. Ready for some kick-ass chili?"

"Oh no! No, we don't! Gwen'll kill me. He gets junior chili with cheese-and-crackers." Hector parked the boy in front of the TV. He went into the kitchen for a dish of plain hamburger and beans off the back burner. Maybe with just a little juice. Not enough to make a mess.

"What are we watchin', pardner?" Terry asked, clicking the channel dial. "Lemme find the *Stooges* for ya. Whoa, there went Santa! Don't worry, it was just a commercial. Hey! Do they still have *Three Stooges* on here anywhere?"

"I don't think so." From the refrigerator, Hector brought cheese cubes he knew Wesley would eat. He arranged a few *Ritz Crackers* on a plate. "Find Kermit or something. Christ, for a second I thought you meant *Iggy and the Stooges.*"

"Naw, man, c'mon," Wickersham said. "I can dig your, you know, domesticity." Staggering slightly, he once again tipped back his Christmas brew.

—⟋⟍—

Saturday morning, Hector's head was splitting. But at least his stomach felt OK. He was able to roll out immediately when Wes padded into the bedroom. Luckily, he rolled his face out into the chill air before Wes came around to his side. He'd slept for a few hours with his face resting on Gwen's abdomen. She groaned and rolled away, half uncovering herself. Hector quickly tugged the blankets back over her. He struggled into his briefs then found his sweatpants and glasses.

"I want pancakes."

"Mmm-hmm. How about frozen waffles?"

At the bottom of the stairs, Wickersham snored on the hide-a-bed unfolded from the couch. Again, Hector restored a blanket over a naked adult. "Don't wake him up yet," he whispered to the boy.

Robin Hebert came out of the kitchen in her wrinkled waitress dress. She carried an empty case for the Christmas lagers. There were longneck bottles everywhere, like poorly hidden Easter eggs. There were bottles on the coffee table and dining room table in profusion. They stood next to the reclining chair and the hide-a-bed. Two full ashtrays on the floor were flanked with bottles.

"I'll get those," Robin said in a low voice. Her short blond hair was slicked back and damp from the shower. "Then I've gotta split. I'm out of cigarettes."

"Who's *that* lady, daddy?"

"Don't you remember me, shortstop? From the restaurant?"

"Is there any coffee? Don't you want some coffee?"

"I think you're out." Robin put bottles into the beer case two at a time. They clanked together.

"Ohhhh, shit," Wickersham groaned. "*Easy* there. Those are *worth* somethin'."

Robin came into the kitchen. She dumped warm beer out of two bottles. She fished out a cigarette butt that spilled into the sink.

"Yeah, there isn't enough. My fault. I had that on my list for yesterday, but…" Hector put the top back on the avocado-tinted canister, the scoop rattling inside. He turned on a burner under the tea kettle. "I can have instant for you in just a minute."

"That's alright. Tell you what. I'll bring back some big carry-outs from the gas station. I have *got* to get some smokes. Then I need a fresh uniform from home. Gwen and me both have the lunch shift. We'll just have to shop tonight. Or maybe Sunday. You remember?"

"Yeah, vaguely. Something else for her to be mad at besides *me*." Hector spooned *Maxwell House* crystals into a mug. His throbbing head could not wait for the gas station coffee. He suspected that Terry would also drink instant under the circumstances. "It'll be OK. By the time you come back, we'll be ready to drink 'em on the road. Terry and I have some errands."

"You *better* go buy her something nice," Robin teased. "With your *porn* money."

"I think she wants one of those *Mr. Coffee* gizmos."

Robin slapped his arm. "I mean for *her!*"

Fritch opened the freezer above the 'fridge to get the toaster waffles. He heard Robin slam the front door hard enough to jingle the bells in their wreath.

"Owwww, Jesus." Terry groaned. "What is *wrong* with her?!"

"I dunno. Afterglow?"

Wickersham sat up. He clutched the wool army blanket at his neck like a disaster survivor. By the time Fritch handed him the steaming mug, Terry had lighted the remains of a cigarette from an ashtray. "She wouldn't *be* out if she'd smoke 'em all the way." He slurped the coffee. "No, that doesn't make sense. She'd still be out. Wait. She wouldn't be out if she went back and… Oh, fuck it."

"Hey," Fritch whispered. "The *kid's* up."

"Oooops. Sorry."

"Figure out your semantics while I get him fed. You want a waffle?"

"Sure." Wickersham exhaled slowly. "Better make it dry."

Fritch hoisted Wes into a booster seat at the dining table. "Jam or syrup, ace? Don't say *both*. We don't have time for a big mess."

"Jam. You look all sad," he told Wickersham. "You need a aspen?"

"Coffee first, sport. I'll be smilin' in a little bit."

"Terry abused a substance, Wes. Can you say that? *Terry abused a substance?*" Fritch brought a plain waffle to his guest.

"Don't know those words, Daddy." The boy picked up his first waffle.

"Not important. Just try to repeat it whenever you see Terry holding his head in his hand. Like now."

"You boozed a stubbins?"

Fritch laughed and got a stab in his *own* head. "Yeah, he did *that* too."

"Have your fun," Wickersham sighed. "And then go eat some….*you* know."

Fritch mopped Wes's hands and face after he'd finished eating. He hustled the boy upstairs to get him dressed. "Better use the john so we can get rolling," he told Terry.

Fritch helped Wesley into a sweatshirt and little blue-jeans. He laced the little tennis shoes for him. "You can practice tying tomorrow. We need to get going."

"For road trip?"

"Yeah, it's a road trip. Not that long though. Not like down to Grandma's farm. When we get done with business, we'll go into the stores."

"Can I see Santa again?"

"Nah, buddy. You have to help shop for a present for Mom. Remember about *giving* and all that stuff?"

"Better than receding?"

"*There* it is." Hector filled a tote bag with diversions: A John Deere coloring book from the dairyman grandfather. It had a few pages left to do. Crayons. The *See 'n' Say* for farm animals. The Wil Huygens picture book of everything about gnomes, even with some gnome breasts showing. "Think this'll do it?"

Wes did not reply. He carried a GI Joe in one hand and a Tupperware container filled with tiny weaponry in the other.

"*Wow*, you've got a lot of toys. Santa might bring you Savings Bonds after all."

—⚏—

Robin rolled up to the curb just as Hector finished strapping Wes into the back of the station wagon. A sparse, wet snow fell as he withdrew from the car. She handed over the large Styrofoam cups of coffee. Flakes turned to dew-drops on her wool hat. She nodded disgustedly at Wickersham's form slumped in the front seat. "Have a great *day*," she called. "Don't forget, you're gonna show me how to mix *Snowshoes* later. I'll pick up some *Wild Turkey*."

Wickersham lifted his arm weakly. He waved without turning or even raising his head. Robin rolled her eyes. "He's doing *what* for you today?"

"Oh, he's my *muscle*."

"You *may* be in trouble. Better be ready to pull over." She tip-toed carefully through the slush in her white, waitress shoes. Gwen, in curlers, opened the door for her as she climbed the porch steps. Both women eyed the chiming wreath with irritation.

—⟋⟋⟍—

Fritch drove the same route he used to go to work. There were lanes through the slush on each side of the blacktop going west to Route 24. Wickersham revived a bit. He straightened up to have another cigarette.

"That waffle was a good idea. I shoulda had another one."

"I think there are some saltines in the glove box."

Wickersham sipped more coffee then searched for the crackers.

"I hope you're not drinking your *Snowshoes* at our house tonight."

Terry stripped cellophane from some restaurant saltines. "I won't be drinking *anything* tonight. Robin'll be *your* problem. She and Gwen liked the idea because peppermint schnapps and cracked ice sounds Christmassy. I need to get clear of it."

Fritch turned south on Route 24. Traffic was slow on the divided four-lane. This was the last weekend for holiday shopping at the malls down in Oakland County. "You're not going to follow up on last night? What's wrong with Robin?"

After a few tentative chews, Wickersham swallowed the first cracker. "It wasn't such a success. She does everything too fast. And I mean *everything*. I was getting mellow. And plus, after a few drinks she never shuts *up*."

Fritch tested the left lane. The pavement was still just wet. "OK. Just don't whine next weekend about how horny and lonely you are."

"I *won't*." Terry ate another cracker with more enthusiasm. "My *God*, these are good! *Never* be without these, do you hear?! Maybe I'll feel better later.

I forgot about New Year's Eve. But, wow, this morning…I know it's rude not to respond when someone speaks to you, but it hurt just to move my head."

"I hear you. She *does* go on. But she's Gwen's friend. I don't have to talk to her most of the time."

"What's horny?" Wes asked.

"It's when you want to see someone really badly," Fritch said over his shoulder. Then he considered the thought progression that might follow from this definition. "No, I'm just kidding, Wes. It's like having a headache, the way Terry's is. Imagine how it would hurt to have a cow horn growing out of your head."

"From boozin a stubbins?"

"The very same thing, right Terry?"

Fritch's chest tightened with apprehension as he drove through Oxford. He might be out of a job for a long time and this was the road to that job. The trip and the assembly-line labor were a hassle, but there was always a decent paycheck. All he could expect today was confrontation and probably ill-feelings. He supposed there might even be violence. Even if the skin-flicks were returned to him intact, they would be worth nothing in the check-out line at *Yankee Store* or *K-Mart*. The foggy gloom of the day did not inspire optimism. If Preacher hadn't already drunk up *his* last paycheck, *that* would be a Christmas miracle. Workers from the eliminated shift could not draw unemployment for another week yet. It took Fritch nearly five minutes to get through each of the three traffic lights in Lake Orion.

"How are you gonna play it?" Wickersham spoke without opening his eyes.

"Civil, I hope. If he hasn't got the cash, he hasn't got it. I'll settle for getting the films back."

"That sounds wise. Especially, you know, with the boy along."

Fritch glanced back and saw that Wes had nodded off. The boy had probably been awake long before rousing his father. "Now, if the *films* are gone, too, *then* we're gonna have words."

"But, *words* as you're backing toward the car, right?"

Fritch lifted his own cup, finding it empty for the umpteenth time. "Yeah, don't worry. It'll just be another in a growing series of *life* lessons."

South of the I-75 interchange, they turned off Route 24. Fritch drove west to Baldwin Ave., then down past the plant. *LeRoy's, The Ventura Lounge, Green Tavern, The Bonneville Lounge, Third Shift*--all the bars which clung to the factory skirts had nearly empty parking lots. Some of those spaces were quite large. Opportunistic bar owners, most of them retired union officials or foremen, rented out shift parking to their regular customers. Preacher could be sprawled across the mahogany in any one of them.

Fritch turned west again on Kennett. He watched for Clevinger's street. He remembered the old man bragging that he could crawl home from work if he had to. What would that mean? Three blocks? Three miles? The slip of paper on the dash with Preacher's phone number read *Carlisle Street.*

"*That's* it." He had no time to hit the turn signal. They weren't going very fast but the station-wagon cornered like a bread truck. Wes didn't wake up but Wickersham came to full alertness.

"Showtime?"

"There won't be any *show*. Relax," Fritch repeated. "Five blocks from work. I think this guy's people were part of the migration during the Depression. Or maybe for the war effort. *One* of the wars. You know, there are still a few of those old boys that commute to Kentucky every couple of weeks. They stay in rooming houses up here."

"Sounds like *my* family tree," Terry said. "Up until Daddy."

The pre-war bungalows were uniformly dingy. All were of one storey with concrete block porches. Half of them had added detached garages. Some were sided in aluminum, but most were slate or shingle-sided to look like slate. Fritch told himself that the weather and his hang-over might color everything. But the weather hadn't put broken toys and junk in the yards or beat looking vehicles everywhere--in side-yards, backyards, or on blocks in the gravel driveways. He crawled along carefully. Cars and pick-up trucks were parked at the curbs in both directions, violating the posted snow ordinance.

"We want 5962. The evens are on your side," Fritch said.

In the middle of the next block Terry said, "This looks like it. A VW in the drive? An old Tempest half out of the garage? That's a cool old ride."

"Yup. The Tempest is his pride-and-joy."

Fritch pulled in behind the yellow Bug. He had to straddle the sidewalk. He set the parking brake. "Why don't you slide over behind the wheel. I'll leave it running."

"Got ya."

Fritch's first impression was that Preacher's home was one of the better kept places. The old man had upgraded to beige aluminum siding. An overflow of material bounty had crowded his car out of the garage, but there were no bicycle skeletons or lawnmowers leaning about in the weeds. When he tried to knock, however, the glass was missing from the storm-door. Rapping on this wouldn't get much attention. He reached for the doorbell button which had been painted over several times. Hearing no buzz inside, he clattered harder on the door frame.

He heard quick steps approaching inside and then the dead-bolt turning. The door opened with a warped, scraping noise. A wiry, scowling young man wearing only red bikini briefs confronted him. A towel draped the boy's neck though his hair looked dry.

"Yeah?"

"Uh, good afternoon. Hope I didn't get you out of the shower. Is this the Clevinger residence? I'm looking for Preacher. I work with your Dad."

"The old man? He ain't *my* Dad." The kid made no move to close the door. His hands gripped both ends of the towel.

"Well, is he around? I've got some business to discuss with him?"

"You, too? Geez-us," the kid snickered, looking over Fritch's shoulder. "Listen though. I can ast him, but he ain't feelin' too good. You wanta step on in? He'll bitch about lettin' the heat out."

"If he's got the flu or something, I can just catch up with him another time."

"Brown-bottle flu, more like." The kid turned and switched on a floor lamp. The trunk of the lamp wobbled on its tarnished base. An amber plastic shade meant to retain heat had been drawn down in the small picture window. Curtains over it kept the living room dark.

Fritch saw a movie projector set up on the floor. It was aimed at a bare wall, its cord trailing toward an overloaded socket. Several empty porno boxes lay scattered. With a delicate stride Fritch had only ever seen affected by runway models, the young man moved toward an adjoining room. Fritch's breath caught. The kid had some kind of wet stain in the seat of his briefs, as if he'd sat in something. He reached up and tugged at a curtain threaded on a plain dowel. The bedroom inside was dark except for a fat candle sputtering on a bedside table.

"Preacher? You feelin' better? Ya'll awake?"

"Jus' enough. Get yer little ass on in here 'n' get busy, I'll feel a whole lot better."

"Well, no, 'cause ya'll got company."

"Awww, shit. Who the…"

"C'mon, old man. It's somebody from work. An' I need some money."

"You 'n' yer fuckin' money. Jus' a goddamn minute, let me get myself organized. Go 'n' make yerself useful, get me some aspirin."

"Gawd." The boy quickstepped out of the bedroom and crossed into the kitchen. Fritch heard the complaint of worn bedsprings. Then Clevinger emerged, blinking at the light. He was still knotting the sash of a soiled robe. "Oh, it's…well, *shit*! Fritch! *Goddamn,* ahm sorry! I done forgot all 'bout you 'tother day. *God*damn it." He hung his head, squeezing the bridge of his nose.

"Well, geez, Preacher. I waited two *hours*."

Clevinger made room for himself on the battered davenport. He tossed a black shirt and a pair of black capri pants toward the kitchen. The shirt fluttered like silk and landed short. "Ah know ah fucked up, buddy. But, now, *shit*. You *know* me well enough. You know ah ain't just but a ol' drunk." He picked through the debris on the coffee table; a rolling device and papers. He knocked over an empty fifth of *Jack Daniels*. His hands shook as he tried to light a loosely constructed cigarette.

"Yeah, I guess I was a little slow figuring that out." Fritch looked away. Preacher's lips quivered. His rheumy eyes were about to dispense real tears.

"What do ya'll think you figured *out*, college boy? All a this *here*?" Clevinger jerked his thumb at the kitchen. With the cigarette finally lit, he sent sparks flying with a coughing jag. "That boy could be my damn *nephew* far's ya'll know. Ain't nothin' what it seems now-a-days," he gasped.

When the old man lifted his feet onto the coffee table, Fritch studied the grimed soles of his stockings. "Sure. Doesn't seem like *anything*. Nothing to do with *me*, anyway."

"Damn right. Nor nobody else." Clevinger rose to peek out the window. Fritch slowly took his hands out of the sweatshirt pouch. He could probably get to the heavy *Jack* bottle quicker than the old man, if it came to that. Better than nothing for a weapon.. A shower began to trickle in the bathroom. After another minute, he thought he smelled shampoo.

"Who's out'n yer car? Ya'll brung some he'p along? Ya'll com'd all the way down here try'n scare a few bucks out'n a ol' drunk?"

"It's just a friend of mine. I came down to finish my Christmas shopping and he rode along. I thought I'd check, see if you had the money. If not, well…"

"Ya'll never even been t' my place before. Ya'll woulda had t' ast around. An' ah thought we was friends."

Now Fritch decided it wouldn't do any good to be passive if Clevinger wanted to be a tool. "It wasn't *hard*, Preach. You're in the book. And a real friend wouldn't stick me with a bad check. So if you can't pay for the films, I'm gonna take them back."

Clevinger puffed his smoke, held it this time and resumed sniffling. He turned away from the window. "Well, ah ain't gotcher money. Guess ah'll box 'em back up for ya'll, you don't trust me."

"I'd appreciate it." Fritch backed toward the door. "I need to sell them some way. And quickly."

Clevinger knelt wearily next to his projector. His nearly hairless legs jutted from the robe, an alcoholic's spindle legs holding up the slack, toneless flab of his core. "Them is some good flicks though, ain't they? That ol' boy Johnny Wadd… He can do some damage." He took a spool of film off the projector. He scrabbled around in the clutter until he found the right container.

"They *are* pretty good. But you woulda gotten tired of them before long."

"Not *me*, son." The old man grinned. "But looka here. What ah said 'bout things not bein' how they look…"

There were six cartons in the stack when Preacher finished and eased himself up. Fritch wasn't going to examine them until he was away from there.

"What things?"

"Yeah, *that's* the way. Them ol' boys on that line… They got a cruel streak 'bout anybody elst's short-comin's 'cept their own…drinkin' an' so forth."

"Yeah, I hear you."

"So you never seen me in a embarrassin' way?" He handed the films to Fritch.

"No, Preacher. You were wrapping presents when I stopped by. Now, have you got a grocery bag or something? My little boy is out in the car, too. I've gotta sneak these into the back." *Never saw him in an embarrassing way?* Most of South Trim Area had seen Clevinger heaving into a trash barrel at some point.

"Yep. Be right back." Clevinger went into the kitchen. Fritch heard cupboard doors slamming. The shower stopped. Clevinger eyed the bathroom door nervously.

"Well, I'll see you whenever," Fritch said as the old man handed him the bag. "I heard we could be off 'til model change in July."

"We'll come back an' build them little compact cars. Fuckin' A-rabs, anyways. Japs too."

"Take care, Preacher. Have a great holiday." Fritch turned without attempting to shake hands.

"Watch out for Smoky givin' green stamps." The storm-door frame rattled shut, the front door after it.

—⚒—

With the films buried next to the spare tire, Fritch woke Terry to move him to the passenger side.

"I see you aren't shot. And you have the porn back. My people have nearly assimilated."

"They've bought into our *culture* alright."

Wesley was awake and studying the gnome book. He accepted, without question, Fritch's explanation for the visit to an unfamiliar city: *business*. With exactly twenty-three dollars left in his wallet, Fitch canceled the shopping plans. Some sort of credit arrangements would have to be made if Santa was going to visit in style.

Fritch cursed under his breath at the thought of Preacher stiffing him, but he had no desire to tell anyone about the old bastard's lifestyle kinks. They'd probably all be hired back into different departments anyway. Maybe he'd even change lunch bars to avoid the drunken advances, now that he knew the geezer was in earnest. And how about that kid? When Fritch thought about him, he soon pictured Gwen tugging her panties up and heading to the shower after lovemaking. He liked that view of her walking away, almost as much as walking toward him, slipping them off.

Traffic moved even slower on the return trip. Thick flurries stuck on the road, signaling a drop in temperature. North of Oxford, there were cars in the ditch. Terry fished out his smokes. He thought they should eat back in

Celeryville. Now he was ready to have a word with Robin Hebert. *Titus Family Restaurant* served the best burgers in town. Better than that heat lamp garbage at *McDonalds*, he told Wesley. After a little food, who could say what he'd be up for? Talk Robin into *something*. *Snowshoes*, though? He thought he might require more healing before sampling the hair off *that* dog.

Wesley finished the last of the fruit punch in his sippy-cup. He thought Daddy and Terry should drink their beer out of big mugs like the gnomes do. And, it appeared to him that the boobies of the girl gnomes in the book looked bigger than Mama's.

Fritch winced at this and Wickerham chuckled.

Reindeer Pause

In the afternoon, Hector Fritch rigged a couple of lines, old anchor ropes borrowed from his dad. He climbed out their bedroom window onto the porch roof then looped the ropes around the chimney. The weak daylight was grey and he could feel the moisture in it. He wasn't afraid of the pitch of the old roof. He'd been up there in August to paint trim around the dormers. It was an old frame house of two stories. The bank made the sellers put new roofing on before the mortgage could go through. It was steep, but the footing was sure. He'd been sober and steady then, as now. But both conditions could change by tonight. Snow would be nice for Christmas, though, despite the danger.

Gwen liked the idea at first. She thought it was cool but then started to have doubts. The plan was to add some thrills to Wesley's Christmas Eve, leave the little boy with magical memories. But then she decided Hector mustn't wake him up, or worse, frighten him. Assuming that he'd even *go* to sleep with a party going on downstairs.

"I'll go up after everyone's gone," Fritch told her. "He'll be zonked out. It'll lodge in his subconscious. Like sugar plums."

Gwen shook her head. "Or, what he'll remember will be Daddy's last scream before he hits the ground."

Hector said, "Not a chance, with my ropes. I'll tramp around. I'll jingle the bells. Even if he wakes up, he'll be afraid to interrupt Santa."

"What *are* sugar plums anyway?" Gwen asked. "If they're too sour, why not just preserve some other fruit? What's wrong with the peach?"

"I couldn't say," he told her.

Hector gave the ropes a strong tug then climbed down. He crawled back in through the French-style windows. No suspicious ladder to set up, but the boy wasn't paying attention anyway. Wes ate his supper at a kid's table in front of the TV. He was already getting worked up when the weatherman said they'd spotted Santa on radar. He wanted to put out the cookies and milk.

"Not yet, buddy," Fritch said. "Terry'll scarf them up at the party."

In the kitchen, Gwen was making up a long submarine sandwich. They'd gone overboard--three kinds of lunch meat, three kinds of cheese. Plus lettuce and tomato, both pricey, being out of season.

"Shouldn't we have chili or something, too?" Hector asked.

"This'll be *fine*. It's too late to put that together." She folded the long sand-wich into some clear plastic wrap. "There's chips and *Fritos*. That bean dip of yours. Robin's bringing some kind of dip she makes. Is it cold enough to put this on the back porch?"

Fritch rummaged in the refrigerator. He took out a longneck bottle of *Strohs*. It wasn't too soon to start with darkness coming on. "Oh sure. It's gonna snow. Should I make a run for more beer? Before all the stores close?"

The sandwich rested on a length of cardboard. Gwen spread her arms and lifted it. "Get the door, would you? I think one case is plenty. Some of these knuckleheads need to start bringing their own."

Since Fritch and Gwen got married, many of their younger friends had not. It was convenient for most of them to know a married couple who owned a residence and could have a party like adults. Many of them could not yet buy alcohol legally. Even Gwen was barely old enough.

"I hope this is a tame one," Fritch said. "Just Terry and a few others. So is Robin coming?"

Gwen lay the sandwich on a battered love seat left behind by the previous owner. It had been relegated to the enclosed back porch. "Yup. After church." She shivered. "She's bringing her sister."

Robin Hebert was Gwen's best friend. The two of them waitressed together at *Titus Family Restaurant*. "Did Terry want to know?"

Fritch tipped his beer. "He didn't come right out and say. He's always glad to see her, though."

Gwen snorted. "*Sure* he is. Because he's a pig. He'd better shit or get off the pot."

"Hey, I *told* him. When I said *pot*, though, the conversation wemt off course. So, who else?"

Gwen went into the bathroom. Fritch heard water thundering into the tub. "Robin's sister's boyfriend. Joey Morton. He's home from Ferris State. Howie Titus might stop by. I doubt if he'll bring his wife. A few of the girls from work. And *your* friends."

Fritch went back to the refrigerator. He wasn't particularly hungry, just pensive for some reason. He studied the rows of beers. The one in his hand was still half full. Did he have time for a nap?

"OK," Gwen called from the bathroom door. "Keep an eye on Wes while I hop in the tub." She closed the door. The old spigots squeaked shut. The tumult of water ceased.

"Say! You know what?" Fritch spoke to the door. "I've been thinking *I* might go to church later."

The tub squeaked again as Gwen slid onto her back. "Uh-huh. Where?"

"Congregational. Where I went when my folks made me go. I can walk from here." He thought about going into the bathroom. Just a pleasant peek for now. The decorative parts just bobbing there in the suds. Not a very *O Holy Night* concept, but…When did that *start*, officially? Could he be a heathen until midnight? "They have a late, candlelight service."

The tub splashed and surged. The drain gurgled. "Just do me a favor," Gwen said. "Can you clear everybody out of here first? The freeloaders, especially? So I don't have to keep entertaining? I'll still have to pile up the tree before we can go to bed."

Fritch glanced into the front room. Wes had gotten up to change the channel. It was going to be *so* cool for him to hear Santa later. "Sure. No problem. It's gotta be low-key tonight. So I don't break my neck up there."

After cheery season's greetings, it *was* a more subdued gathering than usual. Only a few of Fritch's bachelor friends showed up. These were stoner acquaintances left over from the year Fritch quit college. When he moved back home and took a job at the auto plant, he had plenty of money. He hadn't met Gwen yet. All his old buddies were away in Viet Nam or hanging in there at college.

Terry Wickersham was the only friend from high school left in town. Fritch was relieved when his admittedly shiftless guests excused themselves with family obligations. Gwen's friends from work and her boss ate some of the sandwich, drank a few sociable brews, then left.

Only Robin, Terry, and Robin's guests stayed after Wes was coaxed up to bed. Robin went up with him for awhile. After a few drinks, she insisted that Wes must hear *The Night Before Christmas*. Fritch guarded the stereo to make sure holiday albums continued to play.

"OK," he announced, uncapping another *Strohs*. "Who's up for church?" The clock on the stove showed twenty to eleven. He shut off the kitchen light

Conversations in the front room went right on. Rather deliberately, Fritch thought. No one even bothered to make an excuse. "Right, then," he said, taking his coat from the closet. He pulled a ski cap out of the pocket. "Best wishes to all. I'll be back in a few." Now the remaining friends called after him: *Say one for us. Don't get trampled by reindeer.* Gwen made sure the door was shut tight behind him, pushing the bean-bag draft-guard against the bottom.

Fritch took another pull on the longneck. He placed the bottle out of the way on the top step of the porch then put on his gloves. Snow had begun to fall and gather on the front walk. He crossed the street. Flurries drifted through the light at the corner. They clung to him like dandelion fluff. He stuck out his tongue. He remembered that he hadn't brushed his teeth. Too late, if he wanted to make it the four blocks in time. He patted the coat pockets for a mint or a stick of gum. No luck. Well, he wouldn't be the only one exhaling spirits.

Stepping through the vestibule and into the sanctuary was like passing through a time portal. Fritch had to think. Surely he'd been back since graduation. OK, *that's* right. It was when his grandmother left the choir to move Up North. One last anthem and cake afterward. So, *what?* Four years? But he'd never been to the *late* service, ever.

The place was lighted entirely with candles. Real greens everywhere, tacked along the altar railings, the backs of pews. Pine scent blended with the wax. Totally cool. And there couldn't have been more than thirty people. Intimate. No choir for this one. The little flock sang *O Come All Ye Faithful*. Then silent meditation to something classical on the great old pipe organ. The *Story* was the Luke version. Everyone stood up for it. The minister must be new since

Fritch was there last. Or, he might be the Associate. *Stuck* with it, probably, if the other guy worked the big service at seven.

The communion took him by surprise. No time to consider his current fitness, but he didn't want to be the only one left in the pews. The other worshippers lined up in the center aisle. By intinction, the clergyman said. *Another* first. Fritch didn't try to calculate his *last* communion. Dip the wafer in the one chalice and move on. Maybe no one wanted to hang around cleaning up all the little thimbles. The minister dispensed the Host while a Deacon/usher held the grape juice. Fritch was near the end of the queue, but it moved right along. Try not to breath in the guy's direction. Won't see them again 'til Good Friday, anyway. Probably. The bread stamped flat. Some kind of design pressed into it. Too dim to see what it was. A new covenant in My…Fritch wet the Host and chewed, turning. Like Styrofoam.

—⁓—

The last carol had been *Silent Night* of course. He hummed it back down the street. The snow hadn't stopped. There were tire tracks in it now. He could tell where his guests had parked. Even Terry Wickersham's old *Datsun* was gone. The rest of his beer was *very* cold on the porch.

Gwen came out of the den, her arms full of presents. The bottom of the tree had already disappeared.

"Is that all of it?"

"Just about," she said. "His stocking is up in our closet. Don't forget to eat the cookies this year."

"Yeah. That took some tap dancing." Without taking off his coat, Fritch chose a sugar cookie from the plate on the TV. It was nearly hidden by their Nativity scene. "So, no hold-overs? Can I have some of the sandwich, too?"

Gwen went slowly to her knees in front of the tree. "Nope, and nope. They cleaned us out." She shifted and arranged the last packages. "I think Terry followed Robin back to her apartment, though. Some bull about how he shouldn't drive too far on the slick roads. I didn't think he was that drunk."

The cookie was shaped like a bell. It was powdered green. Bite size. He plucked up a red angel next. "Well, whatever works. Listen, I guess I'll go on up. You coming up soon?" Fritch opened the front door and lifted the strap of jingle bells out of the wreath.

"Jesus, be careful up there."

"Absolutely," he assured her. "Bring the mistletoe up, why don't you?"

Gwen shrugged. "Maybe. I've been up since six you know."

Fritch chuckled. "So? I can always finish without you. Bring me up a fresh beer, too, would ya?"

Gwen relocked the door. "You're *so* romantic." She snugged the draft blocker again.

There was just enough light on the roof of the front porch. With all the leaves gone from his two old oak trees, the streetlight shone right through. He secured the jingle-bells to his own belt. His coat kept them from making a racket before he was ready. Where their bedroom dormer sloped to meet the roof line, he would have to step up three feet. He found his ropes there, stuck to the roof. He slapped them together until the snow came off. He tested his grip then hoisted himself up and over the eaves-trough. The roof was slick alright. He wasn't going to make it to the peak without the ropes. And then Wes's room was actually down a-ways on the other side.

Fritch pulled the lines over so he could move up along the angle where the bedroom stuck out of the main roof. There was some purchase there as he braced a foot on each surface and worked his way up. But the dormer ended short of the roof peak. He put the ropes in his teeth and scrambled the last few feet on his belly. OK, but now he had to inch down the rear slope of the house. The safety lines went slack at that angle. They wouldn't be taut again until he made it down above Wes's room. Or fell.

Fritch tested the slipperiness again then committed both legs to the other side of the peak. With a death-grip on the ropes, his butt began to slide almost at once. *Friggin'* gravity. He dug in his heels before he could go very far. The roof of the back porch wasn't much and it was way over at the other side of the house. He'd miss it by a mile if he fell. The back yard was a flawless white. Not so much as rabbit tracks yet. The scars of a garden were bandaged over until spring. Time to call it a night. No sense having a tragedy. Wes would still believe next year. Fritch clawed his way back up to straddle the peak again.

Maybe he'd made enough noise already. He'd made a *little* noise. But he was probably only above the attic at that point. He dug out the jingle-bells and shook them a few times. Lame. What an idiot he was. He hadn't thought it through. The kid's window would have to be open. He put the bells away.

Using the dormer angle again, the rope over his shoulder, Fritch inched downward on his butt. But now the traction between the soles of his shoes and the snow he'd already tramped was gone. His slippery hold on the safety lines *did* slow the resulting skid somewhat. However, when those frozen soles engaged the eaves-trough at the bottom, Fritch lurched to his feet. The lines slipped from his grasp as he pitched forward.

Not enough snow on the porch roof to make angels, he thought. There was enough alcohol in him for other humorous observations, but not enough time. The wind slammed out of him hard. He saw stars as if he'd been struck on the head. Stars, and he heard the bells under him. Those were going to leave a mark. The eaves-trough pulled loose behind him. He heard *that* too. But it likely kept him from flying off altogether, to the front yard below.

Pointless to take a breath. He knew it but tried anyway. No go. Not yet. No voice, either. Not even an animal whimper. He rolled onto his back. Gwen stood in the window. She was wearing a teddy, so there was *that*. She opened the window. And threw up the sash? What was a *sash*, anyway? Fritch thought, but couldn't laugh. "Oh, my *God*, baby! Are you OK?"

Fritch sucked in his first gasp. He raised his hand and made a thumbs-up in the sodden glove. With the air coming back into his lungs, he tasted blood. Must have bit his tongue. He couldn't believe the contents of his stomach had stayed down with that impact. There was just the cookie and blood. With the next breath, though, he tasted the grape juice.

The Mickey

We hadn't spent all afternoon drinking. That only happened a few times while I was laid off. I was still off periodically due to the so-called *energy crisis*. Terry Wickersham and I *did* plan to party, but only because it was Friday. He helped me hook up the FM stereo to the television so we could hear the simulcast of *Rock Concert*. In the afternoon, we rode down to Pontiac to get my unemployment and put in for G.M. Supplemental pay. Wesley rode along in his car seat, but he was going to Grandma's house later. They liked to keep him all weekend.

"I've got a surprise for tonight," Terry said when we were almost back to Celeryville. It started to rain. The wipers put Wes to sleep. The temp wasn't too cold but March could be tricky.

"What? You're gonna bring your own female companionship?"

He snorted. "Your little boarder wouldn't like that."

Terry had stayed over a few nights with Robin Hebert, a friend of my wife's. After a bad break-up, Robin rented a room in our old, ill-heated starter home. Both women worked at *Titus Family Restaurant*.

"That might be fun later, but no. Guess again." He rubbed his hands together, grinning like an evil genius in a comic book.

"I'm stumped. Just don't mess me up for tomorrow. I have to study." I had picked up two classes at the U of M extension in Flint when it started to look like a long lay-off.

He scratched his four-day stubble of beard. "This might actually be *better* for you. Anyway, we should ease off the beers.

"Awww, no," I groaned. "Is this gonna lower my resistance? Am I gonna catch a cold next week?"

Terry sighed. "It can happen, but you don't *have to* stay awake for two days."

"You scored some mescaline."

"Same thing, pretty much." He nodded. "I got us some purple micro-dot."

I glanced into the back seat. Wesley continued to snooze and drool.

"Yeah, I don't know." I slowed to turn east off Route 24. I looked at my watch. We were thirteen miles from Celeryville. I still had to pack a bag for Wes. "I don't know if Gwen'll go for that."

"Well, Robin digs it. I know for a *fact*." Terry cracked his window and lit a cigarette. "Gwen won't wanta be left out."

I turned the wipers up full. The dinosaur ribs of snow drifts in the ditches were eroding as rain fell harder. "We'll see. We should make a beer run for them, just in case."

"Right. And there'll be free-loaders at your door. I only bought four hits." Rain dotted inside the door. Terry rolled the window up to the merest crack.

"It's my stereo. People know I've got great sounds."

Terry snickered. "Dude. People know you can buy alcohol."

Wesley woke up when we swung into the driveway. I freed him from the safety belts, and he scrambled up the front steps. He waited on the ramshackle porch for me to unlock. Scraping and painting would be my first spring project if I didn't get called back to work. Wes went straight to the television before pulling off his coat. He knew how to turn it on.

"Keep an eye on him, would you," I told Terry. "Don't let him crank the channel knob. I'll get some clothes ready."

It was already 4:30. My folks could arrive at any time. Gwen and Robin worked past five to finish their tables. Then they might help with the start of dinner rush. It was the usual countdown to the weekend. To avoid paranoia, I had to clear away any preoccupations before dropping acid. After I brought Wes's bag down, I took my books and notes off the dining table. They were all about Europe in the 19th Century. Revolutions and unifications up the wazoo; principalities and treaties to remember. I didn't want to take any of that along on my trip.

When my parents pulled into the drive, I plucked Wes away from a *Green Acres* rerun. Terry went on laughing at the show like he'd already done his hit. I carried Wes's clothes in the other hand. I hoped to get him out there so I wouldn't have to hear them complain about Terry hanging out. He *was* quite a hippy, at least in appearance. They weren't buying how hard he worked at his father's resale store, or that he, too, was a part-time student. They couldn't get past his long hair and surplus military dress-coat. I said hello and loaded Wes into the back seat. Ma was halfway out the passenger side but eased back in when the drizzle hit her. She looked hurt that an inspection of Gwen's house-keeping must be aborted.

"Be good now, buddy. Have fun."

"He's always a good boy," Ma said. "*Aren't* you Gramma's good boy?"

I didn't hear what Wes said. "He likes *Grape Ape*, don't forget."

Ma gave me the faintest expression of disdain. "Well, of course. We *always* watch *Grape Ape*. What kind of grandparents would we be?"

"Alright, Anna. Let's go," my dad said. He slipped the shifter into reverse. "Let the kid get on with his weekend." He winked. "*You* be good, too."

"Have to." I patted the hood as they backed out.

In the house, Terry had shut off the TV. He stood in the kitchen, in front of the open refrigerator. He had put his tattered coat back on. It still had the epaulettes and a broad, green belt. You could see where the stripes and insignia had been clipped off the sleeves. "We're down to two beers, you know."

"Well, I thought we were tapering off."

He closed the door. "We better make a run. We'll leave these for the women." When he turned, a smile, like cracks spreading on a frozen pond, started toward his bristled cheeks. His eyes shone.

"Did you do yours already?"

"What can I say? I wanta get off while we walk up town."

"Walk? Why would we walk?"

"Well, we sure can't *drive* like this." The grin was there to stay, apparently. "And I wanta see how the town looks. Here's yours." He dropped two tiny squares of paper into my palm. "Just let me pee, first." He closed the door to the downstairs bathroom.

"We're gonna need an umbrella," I warned. I placed the bit of paper under my tongue.

"Cool," he called. "Maybe the drops will sound like percussion."

I opened the refrigerator again to make sure this adventure was really necessary. Sure enough, there were only two bottles of *Strohs* left, out of a six-pack carton. So, including the two loose ones left from last night, we'd each drunk three for the afternoon. Unusual restraint, actually. That's when I had my own devious inspiration. I retrieved the church key from the sink counter. Using the round end, I gently loosened around the edge of a cap so as not to disfigure it. I dropped the micro-dot down the longneck. I watched it become saturated and sink, then pressed the cap back on securely. Now, Gwen should take the first one, in her left hand. I put Robin's further back, on the right.

"Here goes. This feels like a Tolkein quest," Terry said, an adolescent anticipation in his voice. Behind him, the commode swirled and finally choked down. "That may not be a Tolkein toilet, though. It resists a descent into the lower regions of your yard." He giggled some more. "Did that make *any* sense?"

"No. We've got City sewer. But I'm gonna need the *Roto Rooter* guy. When I get back to work."

"Nevertheless, nothing must block *our* going with the flow. The umbrella, please." I handed him one off an empty coat-hook in the utility room. "You know. We could probably snake that out ourselves."

"Please. Gandolf," I said, locking the front door behind us. "No reptile references 'til this is out of my system."

He held the umbrella aloft, admired it, and then remembered to open it. "Right, right. *'Cause that's how Bilbo Baggins is,'*" he sang. "Or, something like that."

Our journey would amount to roughly six residential blocks. Not much of a quest except for the artificial scenery we had ingested. There was a party store much closer in the opposite direction but Terry's imagination was fixed on *Ray's Tavern*, the only bar in the business section of Celeryville. At least it didn't occur to him to march us out to the *Lounge* at *Celeryville Lanes*. That place had bands on Friday night.

The acid had dissolved. I thought I could taste it, high in my nasal passages, between my eyes. It was more like a thought than a flavor. My mouth went dry. I soon halted and stepped out from under the umbrella. Out of the darkening sky, rain pelted all around my open mouth.

"Get under here. Are you mad? You'll drown like a turkey."

The raindrops slowed, teasing me. When two or three had finally splashed on my tongue, I turned my face to the ground. "That was..." But I didn't *know* what it was.

Before long, the way ahead became tunnel-like, and not just because the street was flanked by ancient, towering oaks. The few times I had tried mescaline or acid, the world had seemed to watch me from just beyond my peripheral vision. Why it remained benign, given my tendency for paranoia, I couldn't fathom. But some parallel celebration always seemed to be playing out concurrent with my own. I stumbled and found it amusing.

"Nice trip?" Terry stopped and roared at his lame double entendre.

"These roots," I tried to explain. The streetlamp above the next intersection cast its weak light on a sidewalk broken and heaved up at absurd angles. "They're...everywhere. Look at this sidewalk, man!"

Nearly doubled over, Terry stopped laughing abruptly. He raised the umbrella again. Studying our path, he declared: "We can still *make* it. We'll have to lift our feet."

"Fine," I said. "I didn't think we'd need a flashlight." If I'd had one, I would have used it to sweep our flanks, just to see what was going on out there in the dark yards. It sure felt like we were being watched.

From the next crosswalk, we could see one of the three stoplights which ordered the traffic through Celeryville. But first we had to get past the towering spires of *Sacred Heart Church*. I didn't see any problem up there yet, unless the doors were open. Maybe there was a Lenten function going on. Next week was Holy Week. We'd both been to a funeral in there. The one Bryer girl, Terry's neighbor, and her cousin. They got killed in a teenager car crash. I remembered an enormous crucifix behind the altar; spiked hands and a bigger-than-life exposed heart. I hoped the big mahogany door was closed. We could get past without seeing all the way in.

"Remember that Bryer girl?"

"Please," Terry said, raising his free hand like a traffic cop, or one of the *Supremes*. "Don't. It was just three years ago but...Just, no bummers, OK?"

"Wait," I interrupted, holding up a finger. "What's that sound?"

A rush of water, steady and with the occasional vowels of an old women's bridge tournament, sounded along the curb. We might not *make* it to that suffering Christ.

"It's just a drain. It's backing up."

"An underground river. Wow. What would Bilbo do? Look at all the trash."

Terry stepped back and prepared to leap. Rain pocked the swelling pond around the sewer grate. The drops struck and ricocheted in tiny silver mushrooms. As I looked closer, a small, broken candy cane, its cellophane wrapper taking on water, hooked on the grate. I squatted and reached.

"It's too far," Terry said. "C'mon. You did what you could."

The red stripes were pretty well leeched out anyway. I stood up, not as sad as I might have been. "Let's go on the other side of the street."

We crossed the intersection diagonally, putting a safe distance between us and *Sacred Heart*. I risked a glance. The doors were shut, but I could hear music. Someone was rehearsing a cantata on the mammoth pipe organ.

"I can't afford a whole case," I said.

"We should have gone to *A&P*. Give them *Buckeye*. They're just intruders from another shire."

"Orks."

"Does it count as spring yet?"

"Persons would be sitting on their porches if it was spring. Look at all the shrubs just dripping away."

"You sure don't have any around *your* porch. Because *you* don't wanta clip them."

"I'll get *one* six-pack," I said. "We must be almost there. Look! I'm all golden."

"The streetlamp plus a caution light. It'll pass."

We waited for two cars to splash by. Then we crossed Capac Avenue at an angle. The red neon above *Ray's Tavern* reflected across a puddle at the curb. In another season, it might have looked like a sunset.

The TGIF racket pushed out the doors as we entered. All the sounds you'd expect running together in a surge, like the ringing of slot machines in a casino. The shuffleboard table clacked along one wall, *those* athletes shouting from either end. A woman leaned against the juke box, massaging Karen Carpenter out of its neon speakers. So overwhelming was the noise and our awe, that the scrutiny of every eye as we entered went unnoticed. *Ray's* was a small space, but we fit ourselves into the crowd.

Bottles of every hue reflected behind the bar. To me, they chimed like tubular bells of light. The brush-fire crackle of hamburgers in the tiny kitchen crept into the bar.

"Just maintain for a minute," Terry advised. The tears of mirth on his face may have been rain. The umbrella had sprayed us both when he closed it. "Find a seat. I wanta have a word with Grimy Dan."

There was one stool at the bar. I eased onto it. I forgot what I was supposed to do until the bartender stood in front of me: "What'll it be, Fritch?" Ray's brother, Ernie, opened beers and tipped out shots while the owner flipped burgers.

"Your Christmas lights are out." Behind the spirits lined against the wall, a string of dark bulbs still flanked the mirror.

"Right. 'Cause it's March. What can I get ya?"

"A draft. And six *Strohs* to go. Longnecks, if you have 'em."

"Mmm-hmm." Ernie shuffled over to the tapper handles. Then he lifted six cans by their plastic harness from the hidden cooler. I swiveled gently on the stool so I wouldn't fly off. Terry clutched his stomach and laughed at some observation made by Grimy Dan. He laughed so hard that no sound came out. They stood near the juke box. Now Merle Haggard was picking a fight with someone inside it. Grimy Dan stepped back, maybe admiring Terry's mad eyes.

I don't know how Terry made friends with the same persons who used to threaten us in high school. Grimy Dan wasn't so bad, I guess. Like Terry, he was a few years behind me. Nevertheless, Grimy Dan had been all about metal shop--patching up junker cars; welding and grinding rebar tridents for sucker spearing. Terry was a *band kid*. I think Dan avoided the draft by knocking somebody up. Now he pumped gas and played biker on weekends. He was wearing his colors; a black leather vest covered with buttons and decals. Nobody in their right mind would be riding *this* weekend. Terry was still sweating out Selective Service, waiting for the next draft lottery. Maybe their tolerance was based on weed, or rock music, or hair length. I couldn't explain it. Those bikers claimed to be against authority. But then they were hawkish, too. I just hoped the guy wouldn't follow us home on the scent of hallucinogens.

"No bottles, Fritch. Not *cold*, anyway."

The shell of beer Ernie brought me put on a light-show of rising carbonation. The bubbles streamed at a tempo with the music. I fashioned intricate rings on the bar with the bottom of my glass. Not my fault the foamy head spilled over. Or, that the cartoon napkins were flimsy. I lifted the glass to admire my streaming bubbles, a neon *Pabst* sign as backlight. Ernie paused to breathe life back into a cigarette at the other end of the bar. He eyed me with suspicion. I slowly placed the beer back on the bar. I must maintain better. But Terry had to hurry up. I quit watching my drink and took a sip.

"Did you get *me* one?" Terry asked, at my elbow.

"Did you *want* me to?"

He shrugged and tugged out one of the cans. "He can do it. Ream out your pipes. He's taking over his old man's septic business."

"Who is?"

"Grimy Dan. I told you I'd talk to him." Terry pulled the ring-top. Now there was even carbonation in the air.

"Thought *we* were gonna do it." I looked around. Grimy Dan gave me a three-fingered Boy Scout salute from his spot by the shuffle-board.

"But, right now… Doesn't it seem, to you, like a completely *impossible* task?"

I considered this until the moment began to stretch. Even *thinking* about the digging was difficult. "You were gone a long time. We should get back."

He, too, appeared to be captivated by my beer bubbles and the reflections behind the bar. His shaggy head turned slowly, the smile now wry. "We've been here ten minutes, dude. What's your….*rush*?"

I tried, but could not refuse laughter at his awful pun. My rib cage was going to ache for days. "Well, I *do* need to see what's up with ol' Gwen. I kinda left something in her beer."

The smile remained, even as Terry's mouth fell open. "What now? You did what?"

Suddenly, the prank didn't seem so clever. I had college knowledge regarding alcohol, but Terry was more experienced with chemicals. He straightened and stepped back. The notion dawned that I may have committed some sort of stoner faux pas.

"You slipped her a *mickey*?" His smile was now frozen and scary. "Don't you know she could freak *out*?"

I chuckled, even as seeds of panic sprouted in my chest. "You mean, like, like thinking she can fly or something?"

"I don't *know.*" Terry struggled to stop giggling. He tugged my elbow toward the door. "C'mon. You don't ever *know* what could happen. It's just not cool."

"She's had mescaline before," I pleaded, snatching up our beers. I was leaving most of my draft behind. "She'll *get* it."

Out the door, the umbrella sprang open again. "But it's not actually mescaline, remember?"

"OK. Sorry."

"Don't apologize to *me,*" Terry laughed. "At least you don't live in a highrise. My smile hurts already."

"Well, don't clench up. Just let it happen." That broke both of us up again.

We went up the block before heading north on Culkin Street. We wanted to avoid the stern scrutiny of *Sacred Heart* and the flood after that. But what other landmarks would we find? Our old elementary school and playground might be cool, but we had no time to languish on the swings. The steeple of Congregational Church, where I went as a kid, was lighted by bright beams aimed from the ground. Nothing gruesome there. We trudged quickly at first, or thought we were. Then we slowed, winded as the adrenalin to rescue Gwen fizzled. Terry played air guitar, humming tunelessly until we were in front of the Sealy Mansion.

"What was *that?*"

"Humble Pie. A little prevue."

"Did you ever go to Dr. Sealy? Now *that* women knew her herbs."

"My ma tried her," Terry said. "For psoriasis."

"Sore eyes as is?"

"Don't be a butt head. Oh! Oh! Listen to this: *'I, don't, need, no doctor. 'Cause my prescriptions've all been filled,* '" he sang, plucking his invisible bass.

"I used to work for them. Mowing and trim. Some painting."

"Whata ya mean, *them?*'"

"The lady that lived with her. Mrs. Stutz, her nurse. I never actually *saw* the Doctor." We slowed further. The huge house was dark except for one window in the third-floor garret. The hinged sign in front creaked in the breeze.

"Yeah, my ma said there was something fishy. She'd see the nurse for twenty minutes and then Sealy for two minutes. Kind of strange when she finally drifted in."

I tried to recall if I'd *ever* seen her. "Mrs. Stutz was fussy but she always found a lot of work for me. I dream about that house. Sometimes I dream I bought it."

"You need to get a life."

"*Me? I'm* not living over an antique barn. Let's pick up the pace. Why does it get farther, the further we go?"

"Well, we were stopped for a minute back there," Terry reasoned. "We're on a big detour anyway. In our synapses."

"I wander through those rooms. There's a lot of old junk left behind."

"Just like Bilbo and the dwarves."

"Except, no gold treasure. Just junk. Your dad would love it."

We reached the corner where we were supposed to turn back toward Main Street. Terry resumed bompa-de-bomp thumping under his breath. Down at the end of Frederick Street I could see the porch light at my house. We wanted to hurry and we tried, but it was *still* far away. My fears grew. Or, my excitement. The trees shook out their wet heads on us. A dog barked from somewhere down an alley. I jumped but kept grinning. Then, at a distance, I could see Gwen in the glass of the storm door. She stood there in her underwear, her waitress uniform draped over one arm.

"What in the world is she…?"

"Wow," Terry said.

As we reached the corner, Robin Hebert draped her arms around Gwen's neck from behind. Gwen dropped the dress. She pulled Robin around. With her face stretched by an impossible smile, she kissed Robin deeply. Then they both stumbled out onto the porch. Gwen giggled hysterically.

"*What?* Did *you? Do?* To *me?*" she gasped.

Terry and I froze in the middle of the street. Wisps of fog drifted from the asphalt as the temperature dropped.

"And where's *mine?*" Robin shouted. "This is *totally* unfair!"

Terry moved forward cautiously and I followed. It had been his role in the past to mollify Gwen, to be the chief apologist for my stupidity. I'd done the same for him. He stumbled over the far curb, provoking hilarity in everyone but

Robin. We eyed the ascent of the four steps to the porch. There was no turning back. Terry made it up the first step. I came behind, the girls waiting like an icy summit. Terry handed me the umbrella so he could grope around in his coat pockets for the final square of acid.

"Well, we made it," I said.

"I'm happy *anyway*," Gwen sighed.

Robin moved behind her again, massaging Gwen's neck like a second in a boxing match. "What choice do we *have*, hon?"

And with that, they let us in.

—⋙—

Humble Pie and *Foghat* were featured on the *Rock Concert* simulcast. My stereo held us in thrall. But an erotic conclusion to the evening failed to manifest as usual. We babbled through an encyclopedic format of topics until the sky began to lighten. We paired off with our habitual partners and fell into chortling dreamscapes.

I was able, by Saturday evening, to return to my studies. I retained enough to do OK on the exam, though I couldn't tell you much about the Paris Commune or the Italian Risorgimento today. Years later, that kiss in the front door lingered as *my* highlight of the evening. But a reprise would remain as illusory as ownership of that mansion a few blocks away. Long after the marriage ended, I treasured that bit of brain candy. I assume it's tantalizing nature had some simple psychological origin; something I heard or saw in adolescence; a *mickey* dropped into my subconscious and ingested unawares. Maybe *I* didn't have a choice either. Or, maybe I *chose* to keep it.

Whipping

Gwen Fritch worked the Saturday morning and lunch shift at *Titus Family Restaurant*. The July weather finally turned hot so she had walked the four blocks to work. Later, when she came into the house, the television was off. Hector's car was in the drive, but he wasn't on the couch. She didn't hear the lawn mower running, so he was probably just napping upstairs. Gwen didn't puzzle over it. She drew the curtain in the front room and shed out of the clammy waitress uniform. She turned the floor fan up to high and went into the kitchen. If he drank the last cold beer, I'll wake him up with my knee, she thought.

There were several cold *Strohs* left. She drank one under the shower. For once, she didn't want the water hot. She faced the spray. She parted her legs and made a slow massage with the *Dove*. Eyes closed, she tipped a long swallow. Since their son Wes was spending a couple of weeks down at her parents' farm, she could relax with the bathroom door open. She could maybe even wake Hector up in some more pleasant manner. Wes always came home so spoiled. They should make their time alone worth the aggravation.

Gwen scampered through the front room and up the stairs. A window fan hummed at the top, but the hallway was stifling. There had never been an attic fan to help cool the old house. In their bedroom, Hector lay sprawled in his scivvies. A small oscillator on the nightstand played back and forth over him. It nearly bumped into his half-empty beer bottle. Bedding lay in a heap at the foot of the bed. Gwen stepped over it. She made sure the mattress bounced as she crawled toward her pillow.

"Hey, wake up, baby!"

"Hmmph. Wha…? Wha's goin' on?" Hector mumbled. "You bring home food?"

"Nope. All the take-outs were taken out." She crouched on her knees, waiting for him to open his eyes. "I thought you were gonna mow the lawn."

Fritch opened his eyes and rubbed them. He did enough of a sit-up to prop himself on his elbows. "Wouldn't stay running. Carburetor float was sticking, then I couldn't find the right socket to change the spark plug. Aren't you hungry?"

"Poor baby. What a rough day." Gwen tipped the last swig of her own beer. "Oh yeah, I'm famished. *And* wet." She smiled.

"Your hair is dripping all over."

"Yeah, and it feels good. I sure wasn't gonna use the blow-drier for half-an-hour. C'mon, wake up. We've got the whole house to ourselves."

Fritch sighed and sat up. He reached for his beer. "OK, OK. Let me get my bearings. I just fell…"

"Hey, you know what?" Gwen put her elbows down into the mattress. Still in a crouch, she began to sway her bottom. "The bed's already cleared. Wanta try that *one* thing?"

Fritch put his feet on the floor. He rose and stretched. "*What* one thing? There are *lots* of things to try."

Gwen continued to waggle--provocatively, she hoped. "In that one porno mag you bought by the plant. The glossy one that was so expensive."

Now Hector peered out the window onto the front-porch roof. He couldn't see much of the street through the foliage of their mammoth oak tree. The bottom of a bicycle shot past in the street. "You'll have to narrow it down for me. I have two or three of those and I thought you were pretty pissed off about the cost."

Now Gwen rolled onto her side. "The one with the sequence of pictures, and there's, like, a story? Might as well get *my* money's worth."

"Ah. OK. There are about four stories in each one."

"Where the girl is getting whipped. The bed is bare. That's what reminded me. They've got her sorta…she's spread out to the corners."

Fritch sat down on the edge of the bed. "You *liked* that? You never said anything."

"Well, I guess it must've stuck in my head. Her butt's all red, but…" Gwen's voice thickened. "She had this look on her face. I don't know. She looked like she had, sort of, a goal and was about to have it…"

Fritch reached over and put his hand on her hip. "I'm not trying to discourage you, God knows. But…*first* off, she's a *model*. An actress or something. She's probably thinking about a nice check for doing some extreme shit. And, *secondly*, I believe the rest of the story involved about five guys, and they went at her all night. I emphasize the word *story*. You remember *that* part?"

Gwen covered his hand with one of hers. "*You* seem to remember it. *Now*. I was just talking, anyway. Getting to have time alone, and…Don't you ever feel like it's getting to be a rut? The group part would be…But we could start with the other thing."

Hector stood again. "I'm gonna get us a couple of cold ones first. I suppose…We really don't have any of the equipment; the restraints and stuff. *That* guy had a flogger, I think they call it. Looked like a horsetail? Buncha strands?"

"Yeah. Not like a real, you know, a bull whip. Like for slaves? I don't want any scars."

"OK. We'll see what we've got," Fritch said in the doorway. He grinned, shaking his head. He dropped his jockeys to the floor before heading downstairs. "We can probably make it tingle, at least."

Gwen could see that he was getting interested. She scrambled off the bed. She pulled the chain for the bare light-bulb in the closet. There was a full tiehanger on Hector's side. He'd bought a bunch of yard-sale ties then decided not to teach high-school. After he got his degree, the money from the shop was too good, and he had some seniority. He only needed a few of these. For weddings, funerals, church every few months when he backed off on the drinking. There didn't seem to be any silk ones, though. She chose four of the longer ones then flopped back down on the bed, belly first. Her heart rate was thumping so that she noticed it.

"What? You didn't want duct tape?" Hector chuckled when he saw the ties. He put the beers on the night stand. He placed a paperback *Webster's* under the base of the fan and re-aimed it.

"No. I don't wanta give you any *more* ideas." She spread her legs and reached her arms toward the bed-posts. "I can iron these if you ever need them."

Fritch gathered a couple of foam pillows from the floor. "Wait. Put these under you."

Gwen pulled the pillows under her. "How's that?"

"One more." He found another pillow and she took it. "There you go. Now *that's* a nice view."

"Do I look OK? Is my ass even *right* for this?"

Fritch took a drink. "Well, I'm no expert. But I *think* you're gonna want pictures."

"Really? Aren't *you* sweet. When you want to be. There's about four shots left in the *Polaroid*. I used most of them at Kindergarten graduation."

"That's enough for before and after." Fritch rummaged in the bottom drawer of Gwen's dresser.

"C'mon. C'mon, before I chicken out. I'm supposed to be *bound* first. Then you can screw around while I lie here help…"

"Hey, would you *give* me a minute? You're nagging the guy who's about to have the…whatever I'm using. First thing I'm gonna invest in is one of those ball-gags."

Gwen giggled. "Sorry. Please don't be angry, sir. And I *never* gag."

Fritch laughed and began with her wrists.

She felt a growing helplessness as her hands were pulled toward the bed-posts. This must be when the true panic would start, she thought. If it was for real. If she wasn't among friends. How would you even *know* that many friends? the kind who did these things? Hector climbed over her, brushing across her bottom.

"You're getting *into* this, aren't you?"

"Sure. Who wouldn't?" he said.

"Make 'em a little tighter."

Hector took all the slack out. She watched him make some kind of hitch knot around each bedpost. At the foot of the bed there were no posts so he had to find the metal frame under the box-springs. The angle of her spread feet felt like it was opening her. As if she wasn't nearly there already. Holy crap, was she going bat-shit crazy? Farm girl, *4-H*, cheerleader. Just a few years ago, for Christ's sake. She groaned softly.

"Are you OK? Too tight?"

"No, baby. No worries."

"We don't *need* to do this, you know. Looks like you're lushing up already."

Gwen sighed and swallowed. "I know, but I think it might get better. We probably ruined your ties anyway. Let's see where it goes."

With her hands secured, Gwen couldn't see much of what was happening. She craned her neck enough for a glimpse of her vanity mirror. It was Hector's turn to rummage around in the closet.

"You didn't find anything?" He called. "For the actual..?"

"You've got belts. There's a wide one, but I think it'll leave a mark."

"Anything'll leave a mark, hon. Depends how hard it's used."

Gwen turned forward again and let her face rest on the mattress. "Just seems like it'll hurt a *lot* and I'll wanta quit. You need to start easy, like, so I can build up to it."

Hector was quiet then, but she heard the light-chain pull. Then the floor creaked and she sensed him behind her. "Did your *dad* ever use his belt?" he asked soberly. His voice had lost some excitement.

"No, for heaven's sake! This isn't about anything like that," she sighed and reopened her eyes. "I don't *think*. Maybe on the boys. He was a yeller."

Fritch stepped into her range of vision. "Well, OK. But that's one thing I *won't* do," he laughed. "How about this?" He dangled a blue terry-cloth bath-robe tie in her face. "Huh? How wicked looking is *this*?"

Gwen clucked her tongue. "Will that even make a noise?"

Fritch gripped the belt in the middle with his left hand. This allowed a foot or so of the material to hang from his right. "You won't get much of a noise until we upgrade to leather. Let's see."

He trailed the business portion down the small of Gwen's back. He caressed her rump and then back up between her shoulder blades. "I'm not questioning your skill, sir, but that just tickles."

Fritch paused and she heard the pop of the *Polaroid* flash, the whirr of the exposed film ejecting.

When Fritch again brought the sash down, Gwen flinched. "OK. Now that one just surprised me."

"Hey, I've got an idea, though." Fritch retrieved Gwen's fresh beer from the nightstand. "Ever get snapped by a towel?"

"When would *I* get snapped by a towel?"

Fritch poured carefully, just a trickle along the bottom of the strip until it was sodden.

"Hey, is that mine?"

"Yup. You know. At the beach? Gym class? The usual towel snapping venues."

"Well, no, then. Nowhere, that I can recall."

The next blows fell left, right, left, right; not much harder, but now they made a definite slapping sound. "How's *that* feel?"

Gwen's arms were spread enough so that she couldn't shrug. "Different. I sure know you're there. Maybe just a little harder."

The irritation that began was not unpleasant. Not quite a burning, yet, but warming. "Is it getting pink at all?" She thought of the porno photos again and tried to see how she looked in the mirror. The angle showed only Hector and the backs of her knees. He stopped the flogging and stepped back.

"I guess so. I don't really wanta turn the light on."

The afternoon had slipped away. Being on the shady side of the street, their bedroom was subject to an early dusk. Now Gwen caught a glimpse of Hector admiring his work. He still had his glasses on. With hands on hips, the terry cloth dangled. He was getting a beer-gut. The earlier erection she'd felt had begun to wilt. She giggled.

"What?"

Another peek at the vanity and she couldn't hold back. "Baby...Babe..." Now she was really laughing.

Hector dropped the sash. It lay across her calves. She felt his weight taking a seat by her hip. "Well, whata you *want* from me?" He laughed, too. She heard him swig the *Strohs*.

"I'm *sorry*. You just don't *look* like a dungeon master," Gwen gasped. "I'm *so* sorry. I thought we were getting somewhere, too."

Hector touched her inner thigh with the cold bottle and she squirmed. "And *you* look pretty well fed for a slave girl."

Gwen would have liked to turn on him at that comment. "I *had* a damn *kid*, remember?"

Hector reached under her, the heel of his hand pressing until she pushed back. She lifted and wriggled against it.

The little fan continued to splash the humid room around them. Hector held the bottle for her to sip.

"It still feels warm," she said. "You musta raised *some* color."

She heard the beer bottle clink on the floor. The *Polaroid* burst again, lighting the headboard. His weight shifted and he knelt behind her, between her knees.

"Don't look in the mirror anymore. Try to be serious."

She felt Hector's mouth at the base of her spine. OK. A sort of lashing she understood.

He began to probe lower, then paused: "Hey, you're not *laughing*."

Gwen's eyes had drowsed shut as she dropped her guard. Hector's new approach had taken away whatever interest she'd had in pain. "I'm saving it," she sighed. "For *your* turn."

Keychain

Hector Fritch was not proud that he had wept briefly before passing out. Maybe it started while he was on the phone to let Gwen know where he was. Luckily, it was a slow Thursday night in the drunk tank at Genesee County Jail. He found bench space to curl up on. He had started out with a paycheck in his pocket and an offer to punch out early. Everyone showed up for payday, so there were extra workers in the Trim Shop at Fisher Body-Pontiac. It was his turn to go home if he chose. Between work in Pontiac and college classes in Flint, Fritch didn't have to think twice. He headed back up to Flint.

As he closed his eyes and the room slowly spun, an older black man's hoarse voice told him: "Easy now, young boy. Ever body fuck up now 'n' again."

A few hours later, nausea brought him to consciousness. Fritch stumbled to the seatless commode. He gave back two Coney dogs, a pickled egg, a bag of pretzels, some poorly chewed beer nuts and much of the *Strohs* he'd drunk but hadn't pissed away in the men's rooms of three topless bars.

"Aww, yeah. My favorite alarm clock," another voice groaned behind him. "Wipe that seat when yer done."

Hector splashed his face in a grimy porcelain sink and realized that his glasses were missing. He scrubbed at his gummy eyes with the palms of his hands then dried with paper towel. He hoped his glasses were safe with his belt, wherever *that* was.

"You been through this before?"

The other white guy, who Hector had awakened, now took his place in front of the toilet. He did not answer but held up a finger for patience, waiting on his own uncertain stomach. "Oh yeah," he sighed, after a few unproductive gags. "*Geez-us,*" I need a cigarette."

"So, how do I get out?"

"You make yer call yet?"

"Yeah, I didn't want my wife to think I was dead."

"Sure. Good plan." The man rose by painful stages. "Jus', whatever you do, don't plead guilty without talkin' to a lawyer."

Fritch sat back down on the long bench. The black gentleman snored at the other end. "Even if you *know* you're guilty? Won't it go easier if you don't cause them a lot of paperwork?"

"Son," the man sighed again. "Maybe easier for *them*. You got to plead outta here *not guilty*. First offense, they *expect* you to drop some bucks to get the charge reduced down. It's the *process*. It's how yer legal system supports the lawyers. Anyway, if yer guilty today then you gotta *pay* today. I'm Fred."

Fred stepped delicately toward Fritch, extending his hand. Fritch took it. "So, when do I get out? How does *that* work?"

"Don't you even want yer free breakfast first?" Fred chuckled. He sat down on the next bench. One shaft of May sunlight made it through the dirty, barred windows. It rested on his shoulder. "They'll be along, take us across the street. They already come after three other dumb bastards. First com'd, first served, I guess. You was out cold."

At that moment, a young woman in uniform arrived with a tray. She was armed only with a pair of handcuffs and a spray can of MACE. Breakfast consisted of three 16 ounce Styrofoam cups of coffee and a stack of toast. She pushed the tray under the pen's gate. The bread was barely browned. Even without his glasses, Fritch could see bottom through the weak coffee.

"Leave some for *him*," the officer said, indicating the old black man, still sleeping. "Transportation is due back any time now. Mr. Fritch? When you've eaten, give a holler and we'll process your belongings back to you."

"You transportin' me too, darlin'? Woodley? An' I'd like to get my smokes back." Fred sipped some of the tepid coffee. He eyed, uneasily, the thick layer of margarine on his first slice of toast.

"Why *wouldn't* we transport you, Mr. Woodley? According to your sheet, you *know* this drill."

"Well, it's jus' I told my lawyer between 9:30 an' 10:00 a.m. What time is it ?"

"Almost eight-thirty. You'd better go over and wait in Holding so you don't miss him."

"Wooden benches over there," Fred told Fritch. "Like church pews, but they got some angle to 'em. Better on my back than these ol' planks."

"Guess I'll find out." Hector chewed as he spoke, his first slice nearly gone.

"I wonder who they got sittin' this mornin'. Hope it ain't ol' Elliot. He don't like to *see* me." Woodley took another tentative sip of coffee. He placed the toast back on the pile. "Prob'ly won't make no difference. They read my sheet, I'm in for it."

Fritch struggled to offer some consolation. The man appeared to be at least fifty, but Fritch knew plenty of hard drinking shop workers who were haggard beyond their years. Woodley wore long, grey sideburns in the current rock-a-billy fashion. These gave his face an extra wizened look. "Don't they offer any programs to maybe get you off the booze? I mean…if you wanted to?"

Fred snorted but then smiled. "They was one stint of AA ordered after my second offense. Damn smoke in the meetin' near blinded me. Could use some a *that* right now." He tipped back some coffee after putting the toast down. "Nah. Even if I quit cold, never took another drop, I'm still lookin' at ninety days. An' I don't *feel* like quittin'."

"Geez." Fritch picked up the toast Woodley had rejected. He couldn't help thinking *dumb-ass* about the guy, then remembered where *he* was. "That's a bitch."

"What I didn't tell ya is, I already got me a disability from Generous Motors. Two ruptured discs. Happened right on the motor line over at Cheve-in-the-Hole." Now Fred laughed with a wince. "I can do the *time*, awright. Jus' gotta get my ex t' come over an' feed the cats."

After Fritch had appeased his stomach with the toast, he called for the deputy. She unlocked and led him to a teller's window labeled Property. An officer behind the grill asked his name then retreated to a shelf of filing baskets. This guy wore a sidearm. The basket contained Fritch's wallet, belt, glasses, and a Dixie Cup of dimes, quarters, and three breath mints. The sunlight streaming in was stronger when he put the glasses on. He popped a mint. A receipt for his impounded vehicle lay on the bottom of the basket. "Please check your items then sign the release on the clipboard."

"I don't see my car keys." Fritch instinctively patted the front pockets of his jeans.

"You won't," the deputy said. "You get those when you pay the tow and storage."

Just as he had begun to rally with the wallet in his pocket and the sunlight playing around him on the floor, Fritch's heart sank at this new complication. He jotted his name on the Property manifest then read the bill. "South Grand Traverse. How far is *this* place?"

"'bout a mile-and-a-half. You don't wanta walk it though. You wouldn't like the neighborhood."

"I need you to come back and wait in the tank now, Mr. Fritch." The jailer touched his elbow.

"Sure," Fritch said. It was then that he discovered another missing item. With what felt like an icicle stabbing his chest, he studied the pale crease on his ring finger. There was no way to blame a fellow inmate for slipping the wedding band off as he lay in a stupor. Fritch could hardly pull it off himself. He remembered putting it on the keychain. As if any of the topless dancers cared about his marital status while they gyrated and flirted for tips. Or, had he hoped to get *lucky* in the one student joint he visited? He vaguely recalled a folk singer strumming from a stool in the center of a spotlight. *Hat's Pub*, of course. The walls were covered with all manner of hats. That's where he got the free beer nuts off the bar.

The deputy escorted Fred Woodley out for his turn at Property, then shut the cage behind Fritch.

"Wasn't you tellin' one a them boys this morning, ya'll went to a concert?" Woodley appeared to tip-toe ahead of her, whether from pain in his back or in his head, Fritch had no way of knowing.

"Yeah! It was terrific! Frank Zappa and *The Mothers of Invention*. There were a lot of freaks but Industrial Arena was rocking!"

"Mothers a *what*, now? What the hell is *that*?" Fred laughed. "Way you was goin' on, I figured it had t' be Waylon or Willie.'

"Who's *that*?" the woman jibed back.

"She's just young and don't know any better, Woodley," the officer in Property said. "Sign here."

Fritch pulled out his wallet. He counted the remains of his paycheck. Fifty-five bucks left. My *God*, what had he done? He'd started with a hundred and sixty. In a panic, he counted again, but reached the same total. This despair had nearly eclipsed the anxiety for his missing ring when he came across a receipt from the Credit Union. It was tucked between greenbacks. Sixty dollars paid on a revolving loan. So, he hadn't gone *totally* stupid last night. Maybe his situation wasn't *entirely* catastrophic. But, whether he drove back to Celeryville or had to hitchhike, would now depend on how much ransom the impound lot wanted.

Woodley had smoked only half of his filterless cigarette when two more officers arrived outside the cage. Another coed pair, without side-arms at the moment, chatted with the drunk-tank staff. Woodley sucked frantically at his smoke. The lady jailer unlocked again. A heavyset male officer pulled the gate open. He held up a clipboard. "Woodley and Fritch. Motions and pleas. Let's roll." He eyed Woodley and pointed at a sand-filled bucket for cigarette butts near the Property window. "Sorry, old-timer."

They rode two blocks in silence, from the garage level of the jail to the garage level of the Genesee County Courthouse. They rode without hand-cuffs behind a steel- mesh divider. We must look pretty passive, Fritch mused. Woodley's eyes were shut.

Fritch was called out of Holding almost immediately while Woodley settled in for a wait. The older man staked out a bench across from a prisoner in an orange jumpsuit. This fellow was shackled, hand and foot, to a pipe bolted into the floor. An escorting officer sat out of reach, reading yesterday's *Flint Journal*.

"Good luck, Fred."

"Thank ya kindly. Hope I don't never see ya'll again. In here, anyways." Woodley winked. "An' hey! I meant t' tell ya. Give *my* guy a call later, why don't ya? He'll do right by ya. *Wineglass and Wineglass*. Can ya remember that?"

"Wineglass, yeah. That's *just* perfect. OK. If I can't find one named *Budweiser*."

"There ya go," Woodley snickered as Fritch followed the bailiff.

His Honor, Judge Montford didn't look up more than twice while shuffling and signing papers. Hector stared at the floor and did his own shuffling during most of his five minutes before the bench. Montford read the charge, Driving Under the Influence of Intoxicants, then asked whether Fritch intended to have counsel present. When Hector said no, the Judge asked for his plea.

"Not guilty, sir," Fritch replied, hoping to project something like respectful earnestness.

"And, I suppose someone in the tank advised you that I'm likely to release you on your own recognizance since this is a first offense?" Montford glanced fleetingly at the defendant. "Excuse me, the first time you've been *apprehended?*"

Fritch forced a smile at this accusation. "I hope that wasn't a mistake, Your Honor."

Montford shuffled a few more papers. "You are, in *fact*, released on your own recognizance, Mr. Fritch," he spoke flatly. "You'll be notified by Certified Letter when the Assistant Prosecutor has scheduled your pre-trial hearing. Please be represented by counsel at that time. Bailiff, show Mr. Fritch into the Court Recorder's Office. We'll provide him with a copy of this order."

Fritch took another waiting seat in the Recorder's alcove-sized office. Outside a glass door, the lobby bustled. He spotted a bank of pay phones and realized that he would not have to walk all the way to *Enterprise Towing*. He marveled that he had wasted so much time worrying out the logistics of reaching the impound lot. Their phone number was right there on the receipt. If only the solutions to his other dilemmas would present themselves as clearly. For instance, he now wondered how he could possibly make it into work if he had to hitchhike home without the vehicle. To be missing on Friday night after being let out early on Thursday would not go over well with his foreman.

It took ten minutes for a clerk to call Fritch to take his document. Then he pushed his way out into the lobby. Would it do any good to vow, at that exhilarating moment, never to end up here again? It couldn't hurt, he supposed. He waited for one of the legal- jargon spouting suits or one of the shabby litigants to relinquish a pay-phone.

A gravel voice at *Enterprise Towing* ordered Fritch to *wait a minute* while files were consulted. An insistent headache broke back through his euphoria of freedom. This in turn opened his synapses to impatience. After a long minute, he cursed under his breath.

"You still there?" The *Enterprise* guy finally spoke after seeming to bounce the receiver along a metal countertop. "It's gonna be seventy bucks."

"Well, *shit*," Fritch muttered.

"Yeah. I hear that a lot. Anything else you need to know?"

"OK, but, listen. Let me ask you this. On my keychain," Fritch croaked, his breath suddenly snagged by remorse. "Could I get something off of there? If I catch a ride over there, can I retrieve, say, a *personal* item? I've gotta hitchhike out to Celeryville to get the cash."

The guy at the impound lot didn't quite laugh out loud. "I'm not authorized, guy. Sorry. That stuff's ours until the tow and storage are paid. If the car's a piece of shit we might never *see* you again."

Fritch sighed. "OK. So what time do you close?"

"Six o'clock, pal. You've got all day. I got a customer now." The man hung up with another painful clatter.

Fritch stepped away from the phone for the next desperate soul. He considered getting back in line to phone Gwen. But asking her to come get him might create more problems than it solved. If she wasn't already working the lunch shift at *Titus Family Restaurant*, pulling her away from her own routine wouldn't help heal the situation. She'd expect *him* to drive out of the city. Then both his hands would be in full view on the wheel. He walked slowly down the courthouse steps to the Saginaw Avenue sidewalk.

The new Interstate was just a few blocks from the jail and court complex. An easy start. He turned south. His mood begged for a therapeutic stroll in the fine spring weather, but the day's crisis required urgency. He picked up the pace, scurrying against the upraised palm of a crosswalk signal.

After fifteen minutes of benign posturing and facial expressions at the top of the access ramp, an Olds 88 made the turn off Saginaw and pulled up. An insurance adjuster, quietly intent on getting to a wreck, took him as far as the Davison exit. After that, Fritch walked backward with his thumb out for what seemed like an hour. The spring sun climbed, searing his throbbing head. Then an older man towing a riding lawnmower on a trailer eased onto the shoulder.

Unlike the adjustor, who had kept his politics to himself, *this* guy wanted to talk. Fritch focused on the moving lips as the man grumbled about unions, the Tigers, and the cold spring that had left him with too many lawns to mow all at once. Fritch ate his second mint. He made noises of agreement when these seemed appropriate. Then, to hold up his end of polite conversation, he tried out a fresh lie about his circumstances. He told the landscaper that his transmission had seized up, leaving him stranded at the U of M-Flint Campus. This improvisation was so easy that Fritch threw in a bit about leaving his books in the backseat so he could travel light.

The ride carried him east of Lapeer, past the temporary end of freeway construction. He hopped out at the entrance of a new mobile home park and the old man drove in. The tiny lawns *did* appear to be growing aggressively. Fritch was ten miles from home.

He had to walk some more. An after-lunch lull in traffic was broken by the occasional grit-storm of a passing semi-trailer. Now he had time to think. It might be better to go home with his wallet replenished. He could make a withdrawal at *Celeryville Savings* without presenting his passbook. It was a small town and he had lived there all his life. The bank branch was right on Route 21, four blocks before his house. Then maybe he'd call Terry Wickersham and see if Terry could drive him back to Flint. The guy was always ready for a road trip. If Gwen was home, Fritch could just hold the receiver in his right hand and dial quickly with his left. God, how much easier this would all be if Gwen was at work, and Wesley at school.

Hitchhiking had gone as smoothly as he could hope, but…Now that he was near home, motorists might recognize him. He rehearsed the transmission story again. Before long, a top-heavy delivery truck slowed with a squeal of brakes. As it eased onto the shoulder, Fritch glimpsed the puzzled face of Ray Johns. Christ, *just* what he was afraid of. He covered his eyes against the billow of dust. He jogged past the linen service logo on the side of the truck and hopped in. Johns was a bachelor in his late thirties who drove a local route. One of his customers was *Titus Family Restaurant*. He didn't just drop off the aprons and leave, either. He was a bowling pal of the Titus brothers and sometimes hung around back in the kitchen when he wasn't on the road.

Johns pushed on a hinged lever to close the door. "Wha's goin' on, pardner?"

"Oh, my damn transmission won't shift outta Park. I had to leave the Mercury in Flint." Fritch hoped the story would hold up to a more inquisitive audience.

"Bummer," Johns said, bringing the truck back up to speed. The long floor shift made a little grind with each gear change.

"Yeah. Yeah it is. I sure didn't need this," Fritch sighed. "I had two classes and now I've gotta bring it home somehow then figure how to get to work."

"Don't your wife have a car?"

Wow, Fritch thought. Here comes the uninvited brainstorming. Doesn't anyone just let you *vent*? "That's probably what it'll come to."

"Have you got road service with your insurance?" Johns scratched at a two-day growth of stubble. He wasn't be a bad looking guy. Probably led one of those great bachelor lifestyles Fritch sometimes envied.

"I think so."

"You better *hope* so. They'll want fifty, at least, to tow it from Flint."

Fritch's mood plummeted again, as if he'd actually have to *deal* with this expense. The cover-up story was causing him as much stress as the actual situation.

"Who you gonna have work on it?"

Fritch shuddered. Was there no *end* to this? "God, Ray," he sighed. "I haven't thought about it yet. I just wanta get the damn thing home."

"Well, you *gotta* take it to Larry Hebert," Johns said, as if Fritch had failed to name Michigan's governor. "That's Robin's dad that works there at the restaurant."

"I'll keep it in mind."

The truck slowed and wheeled into a gas station at the village limits of Celeryville.

"I'll just be a few minutes," Johns said. "Two hand-towel rollers to change."

Fritch hopped down the step and out the door right behind him. "I can make it from here, Ray. Thanks for the lift."

"Okee-doke. See ya 'round."

Fritch waited for a few cars to pass then hustled over to the north side of Route 21, the side his bank was on. By now all he could think about the experience, from neon night to squinting day and all the complexities of days to come, was that one dumb act led relentlessly to another. But he had no alternative now but to see them through. Yeah, Johns's next stop would likely be at *Titus Family Restaurant* and Gwen could very well be working. He might relate, immediately, that he had just given her husband a ride and follow that up with everything *else* he'd been told. Fritch just had to have a little faith that she'd know how to play it.

A teller he didn't know forked over a hundred bucks from Savings after consulting with another teller and then checking his driver's license. Fritch figured the balance of his account would also be in jeopardy after he spoke with… Who was it the old man told him to call? Wineglass something? He couldn't help laughing. Wineglass. Hey, Stein would be another great name for a DUI lawyer.

He crossed Route 21 again and trudged up the hill from the bottom of Main Street. A green haze of buds on maple and oak trees provided a shade that would soon darken. The blue sky would come through in strobe-like splashes after Memorial Day. The sidewalk was deeply stained, tossed up here and there by roots. He lifted his feet to avoid stumbling. At the top of the rise, he could see Gwen's car. He placed the last mint on his tongue. Might not mean anything. She often walked to work. He was three doors away when she stepped onto the porch and lit a cigarette. She was dressed for work. Her black change apron would be folded in her tote-bag.

His throat tightening with dehydration, Fritch moved closer. Looking down the street, she saw him approaching. She exhaled a thin plume of smoke. He could only shake his head. He hoped the gesture expressed *no excuses*. "Hey, there. Wes home yet?"

"Where's your damn *car*?"

"I was a few bucks short. The whole system is legal extortion."

"He's still at school. You can call and cancel the sitter. Then your parents are picking him up for the weekend."

"*That's* convenient. You didn't say anything, did you?"

"They didn't ask. *They* think you're always at school or working."

He paused before turning up the walk. His hands hid in his hip pockets. "I *am* always at school or work," he decided to assert. "Mostly. I know that's no excuse, OK?"

"No. It's *not*. And before I even *mention* the money, you had me worried sick. It was almost three in the morning."

"I've worked that late before."

"And you always call."

"*So*? I called." Fritch studied the ground, the worn patches of lawn where feet and tricycles had rounded off onto their walk. "I let off some steam and it got stupid," he added. It was his last defense.

Gwen took a final drag and shrugged. "You've been letting off steam about once a week. Speaking of which, Terry called. I told him what happened."

Fritch reached the bottom porch step. "That's fine. I need him to drive me back for the car."

"How long are we going to be broke from *this*?" Gwen started down, flicking her cigarette butt into the empty flower bed.

"I don't know yet." He slipped his hands cautiously around her waist. "Maybe I can scam some overtime." He kissed her on the cheek and she returned it listlessly. "I'll call if they let me work over tonight."

"I'd *appreciate* it. You scared the crap out of me."

Fritch kept his hands behind her. He kept them on her waist until she turned to go. How well could she feel his individual fingers through panties, pantyhose, the slick fabric of her skirt? Like his own *Princess and the Pea*?

Gwen walked down the street. She hadn't yet smiled. She didn't wave either, but nothing could dampen his spike of relief this time. Leaving her car behind might prove lucky, too, if Wickersham's beater was acting up. All Fritch had to do was make one more trip. Just get those keys to avoid being considered a cheat, or someone who would cheat if he could. Well, he hedged, just one more trip *today*.

Superficial

After we moved over by Lapeer, it looked like the Hannons might turn out to be good neighbors. Maybe even friends. Doc was in Skilled Trades down at *Fisher Body* in Pontiac where I worked so I'd met him already. He waved from the seat of his riding mower, mulching up the first leaves that had fallen. I was trying to assemble one of those metal storage sheds at the back of our new yard. Our garage was still heaped with boxes to put away and I needed to put my own mower somewhere. It was the year after the Bicentennial. Doc wore his long hair in a queue out of patriotism. He wore a floppy leather bush-hat, the kind Dennis Hopper had in *Easy Rider*.

Darlene came over a few days later. Our boy, Wes, was playing with her two youngest kids in a sand-box out back. She brought us a roast in brown freezer wrap and four big baking potatoes. "A belated welcome gift," she said. She stood on the front porch in her bare feet. She was skinny but had an ample bust. She wore no bra, so I tried not to stare. Her brown hair was cut in a shag. It was the first time I'd seen that new style on anyone I knew. She smiled over some stained teeth. "Is your wife home? I should introduce myself."

With an oven mitt in my left hand, I accepted the food. "No, she's still got her waitress job in Celeryville. Would you like to come in? I've gotta turn the cubed steaks under the broiler."

"That's alright. You're busy and I've gotta get something started myself." Now she shifted from one foot to the other like she had to pee. Or maybe the concrete was cold.

"Well, thanks again," I said. "This'll be nice. We'll fix this the first night she has off."

"Great. Well, welcome again." She turned back across the driveway toward their place. "Tell her I'll catch up with her soon."

"G'night," I called after her.

Wes and the Hannon boys were soon best friends. They crossed the road together to the Township Elementary School. And, it turned out that the Hannons had a twelve-year-old daughter who could baby-sit for short stints. Darlene finally met up with Gwen for coffee, and Gwen returned the visit. Darlene borrowed an egg, and then I borrowed a coffee filter. The neighbor relationship was off and running. Doc seemed to work a lot of overtime. As an electrician, he had to be doing well, financially. A new snowmobile on a trailer appeared next to their garage, just waiting.

Gwen informed me that we were going to their annual Halloween party. Doc had wandered over to invite us as she was getting into her car for a Saturday shift.

"Is it in costumes?" I asked.

"Well, of course," Gwen said. "It's Halloween."

"I don't know about dressing up."

"What's wrong with the Tarzan outfits we wore last year?"

I scratched my head and winced. "Geez, baby. I've kinda put on some pounds."

"Well, maybe you should back off on all the beer," she said. "And milk and cookies every night? Anyway, I don't have time to come up with something new. I like my Jane and it doesn't work if you're a cowboy or something."

"No," I agreed. "That would be weird." Halloween was in just another week but maybe I could get out on the bicycle. I'd finally made it onto day-shift, but now there wasn't much daylight left when I got home. "I'm gonna look a little flabby, is all," I sighed. "Tarzan shouldn't be flabby."

Gwen squeezed my developing love handles. "You'll be OK. What about me? Jane on French fries?"

"You look fine," I told her. "I'll have to keep an eye on you."

I *did* back off on my calorie intake. I drank one beer after work instead of three. I skipped the *Slim Jims* on the drive home. I skipped the breakfast burritos off the lunch cart and ate a granola bar instead. I might have dropped a pound or two.

Halloween fell on a Monday that year, so the Hannon's threw their party early, on Saturday night. I pounded a few beers after I was sure the old loincloth would fit. In *my* shape, in *that* costume, I required some lubrication. It was made of leopard-spot material to match Jane's--some bikini briefs underneath for discretion sake. I wore a wig of straight, black hair. The green cord around my brow was supposed to look like a vine. I put on a jacket and brought a folded shirt under one arm. Six *Labatt's Blue* in cans dangled from my other hand. Once everybody got it--who I was supposed to be--*that* shirt was going *on*.

It was dark when we headed over. Their driveway was full of cars and there were cars on the lawn. We met Kirsten and the two boys headed toward our house. Gwen told her what was in the refrigerator.

Gwen looked great as Jane. She was smoking again because of some hassle at work. But, she was finally losing the last of her pregnancy flab after seven years. I wondered who Darlene would dress up as. When we rang the doorbell, there she was. OK: That mom from *Partridge Family*. Or, one of those TV moms with feathered hair.

"Trick or treat!" Gwen called. Everybody hugged. *Hey* now, I thought. *Does this mean anything?* Darlene took my beers to their big autumn-gold tinted refrigerator.

Doc came out of the recreation room, intent on getting hugs from every female who arrived. He wore a black frock coat and an old-time black hat. Not a cowboy hat, but something old. I decided it was an Amish hat. And he wore a white shirt with a western string tie.

"Country preacher?" I guessed.

"Nah, Who'd believe *that*? Country saw-bones," he said. "So you can trust *me*, right? Ooops. I left my bag in the other room. C'mon, Fritch. People will get into it without a prescription. You have to have a consultation, too. Gwen, what're you drinking?"

We moved through the dining room into the kitchen. Bottles were lined up on the snack counter. We were both amazed that he had *McMasters*, Gwen's favorite.

"Can you mix one for Gwen, baby?" He asked Darlene. "I'll make introductions."

We went into the big rec room, past a small group monopolizing the stereo. The place was lighted by about a dozen little jack-o-lanterns. A fireplace took up the far wall. There was no fire, but I could see orange reflections off the back. One of Doc's friends was poking at something.

Doc nudged me. "Check it out. We're gonna have Coney dogs."

Sure enough, I could see a pair of hibachis sitting in the fireplace. Wieners were slowly roasting over coals. A cast iron pot, like a miniature caldron, was pushed to one end of the grill. "I make my own sauce."

At least three people sat on the long hearth, chatting and waiting. One of the women, the only pussycat so far, opened up a family-reunion sized bag of buns.

"Fritch, this is Keith. You might've seen him around the shop," Doc said.

I shook the hand of a tall cowboy. This Keith person had long, curly brown hair and a handlebar mustache. Yeah, I *had* seen him. He was another electrician riding around like a paladin on a cart with coils of wire. He wore a six-shooter that looked real, hanging on one of those belts with all the bullets. He'd draped a leather vest over his Roy Rogers shirt.

"Keith brought some dessert." Doc smirked.

"Hey, *Doc*," Keith said. He gave Doc an annoyed look. "You sure he's *cool*? Are you *cool*, Fritch?"

I shrugged. I liked to think I was cool. I wasn't a narc, if that's what he was worried about. But I was getting a good beer buzz going so I was less prone to be intimidated. "Yeah, I'm *cool*. Wanta pat me down?"

Keith gave me a hard look while Doc glanced back and forth between us. Then Keith grinned. "I don't know. Would you *like* that?"

Doc laughed. "Wait'll after the dessert. You can pat *me* down too."

All three of us chuckled then. "Hey, Doc. These are about ready," the guy manning the hibachi said. "They're starting to split open."

"Perfect. I'll go get the people out of the front room."

The Coney's were delicious, all right. Everyone agreed to have onions on them. I drained another beer with mine. Gwen sat at one end of a huge couch. I sat on the floor with my head resting between her knees. She nibbled her Coney and sipped her drink until the ice rattled.

"Ready for a refill?" I got to my feet. I needed another *LaBatts*.

"Sure. Would you? A splash of soda."

When I came back, Doc was crouched in front of her explaining something about his job or sharing some story that made her laugh. I handed her the drink then popped the tab on mine. The next batch of wieners were ready so people got up to fix seconds. I wanted another one too but thought it might be a mistake. I tipped the beer back. The walls were really dancing with pumpkin light and shadows. Someone started the Jimmy Buffet *Changes in Latitudes* album over for about the third time. At least they turned it down. Or, maybe all the conversations were just getting louder.

Doc finished his anecdote and stood. He earned a final giggle out of Gwen then moved on to another woman. I don't know if he even bothered eating. Pretty soon he circulated back to us. "C'mon you two. Let's go have some dessert."

Gwen looked at me, puzzled, and then at Doc. "What's *that* gonna be?"

"C'mon. You'll see. Make you feel real good."

"Well…"

We helped her up, one of us for each hand.

"Is this illegal?" Gwen asked. " Or addictive?"

"Oh, absolutely. But no. This is a one-time deal. Unlikely we could score any more out this way even if we could afford it."

We followed him back through the kitchen and dining room. Keith and a few others were waiting in the huge master bedroom. Two other guys and their wives or girlfriends or *somebody's* wife or girlfriend had joined them. I didn't see Darlene.

"Have you ever *tried* coke?" Keith asked. He was already arranging the powder on the glass of a lamp table. The lamp was dimmed but still reflected around the white lines.

"Can't say I have," I said. "Are you sure this is good? I mean, it hasn't been stepped all over with baby laxative or something?"

"Well, listen to *you*," Keith said. "It *better* be primo, for the money. I trust my guy. I've tried it a couple of times."

He showed us how, followed by Doc. Of course they had to use a rolled up bill of some denomination. There were wide, clear soda straws laying there, too, for we amateurs. One of the women tried it but the husbands were still unsure. I hit it hard just to get it over with. I'd done the snorting thing back in college--what was supposed to be amphetamine: Basically just crushed up capsules called *Christmas Trees* like truck drivers used. Now there was a *head rush*--what we used to call it; an instant cotton wad between my eyes, but a sustained jolt of clarity, too. I didn't know if I could even gauge the high after five beers. The stuff was probably wasted on me.

Gwen bent over the table with a straw as I backed out of the room. I weaved into the hallway. Luckily, I had used the bathroom before and knew where it was. I went in and closed the door. I found the light and lifted the seat just in time. Everything came up; acid-hot and red. Well, the onions weren't red. Then I went deeper, wishing the light was off. I sank to a knee. I laughed at myself between spasms of retching. The muscles in my jaw could not resist smiling, but it felt like breaking through a plaster mask. I perceived all of this in high resolution. Maybe it *wasn't* wasted, I thought, and laughed again.

"Hey Fritch!" Doc pounded on the door. "Hey, man! You OK in there?"

The handle took forever to reach. I flushed, but nothing went down. I heard the water rising and a slow eddy near the rim. "It's unlocked. There's something wrong with your shitter."

—⟋⟍—

They covered me up on the leather couch in the deserted front room. The leather was cold, blissful against my face. Much later, Gwen guided me back across the yard. A light frost had formed.

"Sorry," I mumbled. "Too much beer before."

"It was nice, but nothing spectacular," she said. "Didn't last long enough. Maybe I didn't do it right. I only hit it a couple more times. Yeah, I think you're right about the alcohol, though. Geez, *listen* to me! I can't shut up!." She giggled.

"I'll bet Doc was pissed. I can't believe I plugged up their toilet."

She let us in. "He just got out the plunger, calm as could be. He was too stoned to be angry. He wasn't gonna be mad at *you* no matter what." She went to make sure all the kids were tucked in. I remembered to take some aspirin and then crawled between the sheets in my loin cloth. She must have walked Kirsten home. I slipped into plotless dreams and she didn't try to wake me.

In the morning, I didn't feel too bad. A minor headache and my abs hurt from heaving. The boys were watching TV already. Gwen said *good morning*. She dumped cereal into bowls and called for Wes to set up TV trays. When she came back into the kitchen, I was pouring my first cup of coffee. She dropped bread into the toaster.

"You feeling alright?" She brought the soft margarine out of the 'fridge.

"Not so bad." I pulled a stool out and sat at our snack counter. I heard coffee pouring again and the tinkle of her spoon.

"Listen, Hector," she began, then paused. She slurped. "What do you think of Darlene?"

I shrugged. "She's OK, I guess." There was a pattern in the Formica of the counter-top that I hadn't noticed before. Black, grey, and white splashes. For the first time, I saw that these repeated at regular intervals from point to point. "She's kinda bossy towards Doc. She's got seriously stained teeth, too. From all the smoking"

Gwen snorted. "Yeah she *does* get on him. With good reason, probably. But that about her teeth, though… Aren't you being kind of…what? Don't you think that's kinda shallow?"

I took a sip as the toast leaped. Her knife scratched the margarine onto it. I studied the recurring flecks in the Formica. Every size and shape repeated. "So? Maybe. I know I can be superficial about that stuff at times. *It's* a fault. Her *hair's* cute."

Gwen handed me two slices on a plate. "I guess I'm not, so much. You know…superficial. Not like I might have been."

"Why? I never thought you *were*," I crunched my toast, chewing carefully. I wondered if it might have been smarter to eat it dry. "So why'd you decide you're *not?*"

Gwen swallowed and washed hers down. I heard her gather a deep breath. "Well. Turns out, Doc isn't circumcised."

When I looked up, she flashed an embarrassed grin.

"Oh?"

Now she pressed against the counter across from me. "He's such a hound, too. With *all* the women. So polite and… Anyway, Darlene really likes you. We kinda owe you one. But you need to avoid the coke."

My next bite went even slower. The kids hooted at something on the TV. How had they found cartoons on a Sunday? How could I get them out of there, out to the sandbox or something? "So that wasn't unpleasant?"

Gwen reached across to run her fingers through my snarled, morning hair. "Oh, it might take a *little* getting used to. Superficial or not."

Subsidy

G wen Fritch stood fixing her makeup in the mirror. She wasn't all dressed up--just shorts. But she had on one of her cutest summer tops. Hector wandered up and down the hallway, past the brightly lighted bathroom. Normally, he wouldn't consider going out on a Sunday evening himself. Even though, one good thing, he didn't have to be up for work in the morning. He was laid-off from the car plant and their boy, Wes, was visiting his grandparents down on the farm. But now Gwen was going out.

"You look nice."

"Thanks." She fussed with her dark auburn hair, which had been cut very short. Someone had finally talked her out of the wigs she liked to wear for waitressing. She fretted that her hair was thinning on top.

"Lucky guy."

Gwen snorted. "There's no *guy* tonight, Heck. I'm meeting Diane. We're going to have a drink at *Hoe-Down*."

Fritch moved down the hallway again. He made it to the front room. He knew there was nothing on television. The Tiger ballgame was over. There might be pre-season football later. "OK. Whatever you *say*," he called. He couldn't keep the out the sarcasm.

"Hey!" Gwen yelled back. "Don't blame *me*! Opening things up was *your* big idea. *You* don't have to stay home."

Fritch dug through the Sunday *Flint Journal*. The TV listings were buried in with the coupons, pizza flyers, and glossy furniture ads.

"I'll be out of here after next week," she continued. "So it won't bother you." The toilet flushed.

Gwen had found herself an old apartment in town. All their experimenta-
tions had finally led to a trial separation. She came into the dining room. "That
guy wants to put down new carpeting. The last tenant was a stoner with a dog."

"Well, I'm stuck here," Hector said. "I'm flat-ass broke and I've only got
three more unemployment checks."

Gwen picked a jacket out of the closet. It was denim with a pattern of
rhinestones across the chest. These had been put on, homemade, with a device
she ordered from TV. "Well, the new plant'll open next month, right? You get
to stay with the house 'cause I can't afford it. What else do you *want* from me?"

That's how they had worked it out, so that Wes could keep going to the
grade school across the road. But his lay-off was nearing a year and GM still
hadn't called him back. And when did she start listening to country? He thought
Hoe-Down Roadhouse was kind of a snake pit. That place was open on Sunday
night? "I didn't know you liked that music."

Gwen checked her purse for keys. She draped the strap over her shoulder
and carried the jacket. "Diane likes it. The bass player, anyway. Some of it's all
right."

OK. Let's see…Sunday Night. There it was on the third page, New England
against the Giants. Monday Night Football on Sunday night. Well, the announc-
ers needed practice too. Maybe not Cosell. He liked the Giants because of
that Fred Exley book. Frank Gifford doing the game. Frank's old team. Maybe
he should go out too. All the way to Flint, though? Only bars where he ever
had any luck. Or nearly. He never had *much* luck. Trolling, anyway. A phone
number now and then. That one chubby girl in *Palace Garden* who asked him to
dance. Drunk. She wanted to talk about getting molested. Her own father, for
Chrissake. Different for women going out. Gwen for sure. Always the *object*.
Pursued. Well, maybe not literally. How 'bout *sought after*? Gwen wouldn't have
to buy any drinks. Maybe the first one. No woman had *ever* bought him a drink,
like, to send one over.

Gwen came into the front room. She gave him a peck on the cheek. "Cheer
up. You're just having a dry spell."

Fritch thought she smelled terrific. Something new and spritzed on heavy.
"Have you got any money?" he asked.

She stood in the front doorway, already eyeing the road through the screen.
"Not much. I've been holding back some tip money for school clothes."

"I don't need *much*." Fritch looked up from the TV schedule. He scratched his chin. He'd need a quick shower and shave. The impulse was on him strong, not to be left out. "I can pay you back Wednesday."

Gwen sighed and pushed the screen open. She stepped onto the porch. "It's in my top drawer. But I absolutely need it back if you expect me to keep doing my share."

Fritch unpiled the newsprint off his lap. Going out was probably crazy. A waste of time. But he'd feel better for a little while. At least while he was out. He took her place in the doorway. "Absolutely. I'm gonna sell blood again this week. And the neighbors said they'd buy our extra food stamps at the end of the month."

Gwen climbed into her red Chevette. It was the one *not* using oil yet. His silver-grey one had a black stain around the tailpipe. "Don't wait up," she called. "And lock up if you go out."

It seemed like to Fritch that she backed out awfully fast. He wondered if she even looked as she whipped onto the blacktop. She didn't wave, just put it in drive.

—〰—

The top drawer was her underwear drawer. Fritch had been in there before. That's where she stored some valium. And, he kept an eye on her underwear, to see if she bought any new ones not meant for him. The jar was like an olive jar or something, laying on its side. Just the right size for half-dollars. She must have been saving those whenever a customer left one. Quite a stack. If he took five bucks for gas and five for draft beers…He could sit for quite a while if he just sipped. He counted out twenty half-dollars. Plenty left. He could pay her back out of his next plasma deal. The house payment would eat up his unemployment. But the Credit Union by the old plant let him slide a couple of weeks on the car. Hell, they didn't *want* it back at this point. Twenty of the half-dollars should be plenty.

Then Fritch spied an unfamiliar box under some bras folded in on themselves. He lifted it free. Well, *that* was weird. Condoms. The good kind, too, with scented lube. Why in the world did she need condoms? Only a couple of years ago he had paid for her to have a tubal. Insurance wouldn't cover it. Probably a good idea, though, if she didn't know a guy. That had to be it. But how 'bout ol' Gwen?! He read the outside then looked in the box. More math. It looked like about six missing. Wow. But give her the benefit of the doubt. Could be a few in her purse. Maybe all of them. Or none, depending on how pissed off at him she actually was. But, wow.

Fritch replaced the carton back under the bras. He twisted the lid off the olive jar again. He poured another fistful of the heavy coins.

Buffet

Hector Fritch has suffered worse hangovers--the kind when he couldn't look at the empties; the kind when he didn't know where his car was. Usually, he could settle himself on or in front of the commode, sip a taste of coffee, and begin to anticipate survival. This one features just a little nausea. One little unproductive retch before sitting down. His head isn't *too* bad because he remembered to take aspirin last night. His most pressing concern is that something seems to be grinding at his rectum. Something that feels like dental pumice. And, someone is already knocking on the bathroom door.

He is *up north*, which, in Michigan, means anywhere above Bay City. He has arrived in Lewiston, along with his brother, parents, and much of the Fritch family tree, for a Golden Wedding Anniversary. His grandparents are renewing their vows later in the afternoon. Their retirement home on East Twin Lake and another nearby family cottage is full of relatives. Others are taking up local motel rooms.

"Gimme a second," he groans. With one elbow on his knee to support his head, Fritch weakly tugs free a wad of toilet paper. Taking a peek may tip the balance in his stomach, but he thinks maybe he should check for blood. He didn't drink anything out of the ordinary, that he can recall. Or, that he can recall this early in the process. Even the two *Boilermakers*, downed in macho ritual, wasn't a stretch for him. But, now, what the *hell* did he eat?

—⟋⟍—

The evening's events had been predictable, beginning from when he picked up his son, Wes, at the apartment of his estranged wife. The drive north past Bay City, then through Pinconning and Mio, took three hours. Cool August showers followed them, reminding him of the fall hunting trips of his youth. They stopped to buy the traditional gifts of cheese and jerky, but Fritch told the boy *no* to *McDonald's*. At the back of his mind, an anticipation for reunion carousing had germinated. It had been ever thus with these gatherings and *he* was the eldest cousin. If *he* still felt like partying, how could the younger, wilder hairs be any less so? And, how could they start without him?

Sure enough, Fritch found his grandmother and his parents babysitting some little second cousins. After hugs and handshakes, he saw that a supper of simple children's fare, hot-dogs and *Spaghetti O's*, was just being laid on. "You remember Todd and Danielle don't ya, buddy?" He nudged Wes toward the table.

"Yeah, barely."

"Where's Gramps?" Fritch asked.

"He and Uncle Clay took a couple of the kids fishing," his father said.

Fritch scowled. "In this weather?"

"Well, if they want to go, you've gotta take them." His father began packing tobacco into a pipe. "Before they become teenagers."

"I suppose. But where is everybody else?" Fritch had made no move to take off his jacket. "*Talley's* or *The Annex?*"

"Neither," his father said. "Go back out to the stoplight at County 16. That big bar and restaurant next to the new motel. It's all owned by the golf resort."

Fritch pushed a chair under Wes as his grandmother brought the boy a plate. "Well, *that's* different. It's always *Talley's* at deer season."

His father was ready to step outside. "Your cousin Terri started working out there after she and Ben moved up. There's a band they like and some kinda buffet special."

"Wow. Well, OK," Fritch said. "I could get down with some buffet."

"I think they have *tables* you can use." His grandmother winked.

From the living room, his mother glanced up from some embroidery work. "You guys must have more money than sense. Your Grandma had a huge roast thawed out."

Fritch eyed the door then hugged his Grandma again. "Well, she shouldn't have to cook, *anyway*. This is *her* weekend, right?"

"It's not a problem," she told him. "It's in the slow-cooker. It won't go to waste."

Fritch stepped onto the threshold and pushed out. "Behave yourself," he told Wes. "Don't go in the rowboats without a life-jacket."

His father's pipe smoke already hung on the cool, damp air, mingling with the ubiquitous pine scent. "I'll walk down to the dock with them," he said, darting his eyebrows at the scene indoors.

—⟶

Fritch cruised back through the village. The bars and two motels along the broad main street were busy, even in the rainy weather. He'd never seen it otherwise, in high summer, deer season, or the snow-mobile invasion which kept the town alive during winter. Tourist traffic crawled. A softball tournament, field lights ablaze, added to the congestion as games persisted through the intermittent drizzle. He passed the gift shop where his grandma worked part-time wrapping souvenir coffee mugs in tissue and ringing up the rubber tomahawks made in Japan. He took a right at the light, heading east toward the desired crossroads.

The parking lot of the bar/restaurant was nearly full so he parked out at the puddled edge. He hopped the shallow puddles between rows of vehicles. A stuffed black bear standing on hind-quarters startled him when he reached the shelter of the foyer. Departing patrons, sated with drink and smorgasbord, let rollicking noise out of the place. Aromas, smoky and pungent, escaped as well. A file of the still-famished peered through interior glass doors as a hostess added names to a clipboard. The stoic head of an elk loomed over his right shoulder.

"I think my party is already inside," he told the hostess. "Can I take a quick look?"

"Sure, go ahead," she said. "But it's standing room only at the bar if you don't find them."

Fritch wedged his way in. He paused at the hostess station to peruse the cavernous, babbling room. Then, from several tables pushed together near the postage-stamp dance floor, he heard a chorus calling his name. Patrick and his wife, Carrie, and at least two cousins had risen to wave for his attention. He made for this assemblage by a circuitous route, which brought him alongside the astounding islands of the buffet. He nudged his cousin Terri who was refilling the salad lettuce from a huge stainless bowl.

"Hey, *you!*" She called after him.

"*Here* he is!" Patrick declared. "*Brother* man!"

"It's about time!" cousin Denny Burdette cried, slapping a handshake into Fritch's palm. The grip had a rough-carpenter's callused strength. "You get lost?!"

"My *man*," greeted Mick Burdette. "You've got some catching up to do!"

"Won't take *this* hombre long." Cousin Stan poured the last of a pitcher into a fresh stein. Fritch did a double-take to see that it was actually the eldest of the Brauskas clan. The kid wore tinted specs, a black cowboy hat, and a leather vest over his flannel shirt. Fritch's aunt Muriel had married a plumber of Slavic descent. The Brauskas's were his youngest cousins but Stan now sported a scraggly beard. All the other wives and husbands who'd married into the family added their *welcomes*. Joanne Burdette, Denny and Mick's youngest sister introduced her fiance. Terri's husband Ben, always quiet, also extended his hand.

"Hey! We need another round over here!" Stan yelled. "Why don't they let Terri cover us?"

Denny leaned toward Stan to make himself heard. "We *tried*. What part did you not understand?"

"In charge of the buffet is a big step up," Ben said, too softly to be heard very far.

Stan raised the empty pitcher and waggled it to get the attention of a passing barmaid. "Well, *this* shit isn't gonna work," he grumbled. He scraped his chair back. "I'll try the bar. See if we can get this straightened out." He turned and began working his way through crowded tables.

Fritch nudged Patrick. "What's *his* deal?"

"Some kinda Hank Williams Jr. phase."

"Wants to get there quick," Denny said, raising his glass. "And stay a long time."

Fritch sipped. "Sad. The boy used to look like one of the *Monkees.*"

"I don't think it was Davy Jones, either," Mick added.

Patrick leaned closer. He spoke toward his lap to keep his words at their end of the tables. "Loaded up the juke box as soon as we came in. Said he needed to get an *outlaw attitude*. We *told* him it was gonna get too loud to hear once dinner hour got rolling."

"I think they shut it off when the band was doing their sound check," Denny chuckled. "Never turned it back on."

"Cheers!" Mick raised *his* glass. "To *all* my rowdy friends!"

"Aww, this could get gruesome," Patrick said, then drank.

Stan returned with two pitchers just as their server was finally able to bring her order pad. "Hi, Ben! You guys ready to order?" She had to shout above the racket.

"I think so."

"Where ya been hidin', darlin'?" Stan glared. As he lowered the pitchers to the table, foam and beer slopped over, flooding between empty glasses and napkin-swaddled silverware. "Shit! See, now we need a rag, too!"

"We all want the buffet, right?" Ben spoke at his loudest pitch.

"Sis says that's the best deal," Denny said, now staring his own daggers at Stan.

The waitress counted heads around the table. "So, twelve for buffets?!"

Mick, too, numbered around with his index finger. "Yup. Nobody in the can, that I know of."

"How 'bout a damn rag first, eh hon? An' *these* two ladies here want somethin' besides beer. *Then* we need us about six shots a *Jack*! Maybe some *Boilermakers'll* get these wimps fired *up*!"

Patrick's wife and Stan's sister, Jen, added their orders, eyeing Stan nervously.

The waitress scribbled, her smile gone. "You can all go ahead and get started. I'll be right back."

Fritch drank deeper to hide his embarrassment behind the stein.

"Never mind that rag," Denny told the waitress, pushing his chair back. He stood up just as Stan was trying to sit back down. He took hold of Stan's leather vest at the collar and lifted him in one motion onto the table. The table wobbled slightly but only one glass tipped as he planted his cousin firmly onto the spill. Stan's cowboy hat fell askew but Patrick reached from the other side to catch it.

"What in the fuh…! What're you…?"

"Listen to me," Denny growled. He forced a congenial smile, then pressed his face close to Stan's ear. "Do *not*…" He tightened his grip for emphasis.

"Do *not* get us 86'd out of here! See that biker guy our waitress is chatting with?" He turned Stan's head toward the pick-up station at the end of the bar where the girl conferred with Terri and one of the managers. This gentleman, too, wore a leather vest and appeared to weigh about 300 pounds. "If this works, *that* dude won't feel the need to do a dance on your head out in the yard. Understand me?"

"Yeah. Yeah, sure Den. You didn't need to…"

Denny retightened his hold on the vest, lifting firmly under Stan's chin. "Good. Good. You think you got all that mess soaked up yet?"

"Yeah," Stan squeaked. "Gonna look like I pissed myself."

Now Denny relaxed. He let go of the leather, smoothing the garment back in place. "It's dark in here. Everybody's getting loaded. You won't be the only one." He helped Stan off the table. "Also, you run your own tab. Make sure those shots are *on* it."

Fritch drained his glass. He breathed shallow, wondering if the confrontation would flare again after Stan had stewed for a bit. It *was* kind of humiliating, but Jen ducked under the brim of her brother's hat to whisper something harsh in his ear. Stan sat back, crestfallen. The waitress brought the tequila shots the women had ordered. Fritch lifted a pitcher and poured for himself first, then for Stan. "Easy does it, partner."

The young man frowned at him for a split second then sat up straight and lifted the glass. "Sure. Sure," he croaked. "Sorry, fellas. Hey, I'm just…"

"Just slow *down*," Jen said.

"Right. Got it." Stan took a sip.

"Hell, let's have *fun!*" Denny reached to pat Stan on the shoulder. "We don't ever get to see everybody!"

"Hey, what are we *waiting* for?!" Mick cried. "Let's get to it!"

"I hear *that!*" Patrick pushed his way up too.

Fritch wriggled out of his place, drinking as he stood. The waitress approached again with a round tray of shot glasses.

"Food first, you knuckleheads," Denny said, angling toward the nearest buffet island. "Chew it up good too, in case you gotta see it again!"

—⁓—

Fritch didn't start with salad. He went straight for the hot bar. Some German potato salad; hot, with a vinegar tang rising to his nostrils; the bacon in big chunks; some kind of green spice or garnish in there. Potatoes to soak up some of the... Mustn't forget one of those dark, crusted rolls, same principle. Geez, and look at those broasted chicken breasts. One of those. And the green beans long as pencils, whole and shining with butter sauce. Don't take up *too* much space because... *There* it was, their big-assed meatloaf. Had to be three inches thick in the baking pan. Not too much catsup on top either. He hated that. Then, as he pried out a slab with the serving lifter and found a spot on his plate, he saw the shrimp. Down at the end of the entrée island, the pile rose like a science fair volcano. Could that whole thing be made of shrimp? Crap! And he had no more room on his plate. He looked closer. No. Somehow they'd been arranged upon a Matterhorn of crushed ice. Well, he'd be back. He'd come straight to this end and work the opposite way. He was just getting started.

Talk at the table was now muted by chewing. Fritch made a conscious effort not to bolt his food. That's how you got your money's worth at a buffet. Take your time so you can sample everything. Chewing, like Denny said, sure, but to fit everything in, not just as a precaution for too much alcohol. However, the beer continued to sluice. He sipped between each bite. Stan interrupted his own gorging to carry empty pitchers back to the bar. Fritch looked around, chewing some of the hard roll with a forkful of steaming white-meat. No one else noticed as the kid, still wearing his hat, turned on some charm. With apologetic smiles, he groveled his refill order. Fritch was relieved when the barmaid smiled back. The burly manager nodded and went off to other tasks.

So fastidious was Fritch with his first course that several of the other men got up to get clean plates before him. "Check out the prime rib," Patrick said as they passed, coming and going.

Yes, he'd seen the prime rib with its own little cart and heat lamps just beyond the hot-bar. A young man in a white smock and chef's headgear stroked a carving knife down a round whet-stone. Customers waited in line like papal supplicants until he resumed slicing the pink-centered joint. Its steam and aroma rose through the yellow glow of the lamp but Fritch was not to be deterred. He took six of the plump crustaceans, cold and firm off the mound of ice. He added a gravy spoon of red sauce to the edge of his plate, then more of the potato salad. And, oh! Better get some of that macaroni and cheese. The macaroni was fat and succulent in its own way, not like the kind he served himself from a box at home. The cheese was baked crispy on the surface just like back in school.

Fritch bit into the first shrimp. It was a delight--not too fishy, the sauce just tangy enough and the flesh so cold that it crunched when he chewed. He set the tails aside, wiped his fingers on a paper napkin. He drank and ate, drank and chewed. At some point, Denny decided that they'd eaten enough to permit the *Boilermakers*. He dumped his *Jack* into a half-full stein, then knocked the whole thing back. "*Oh,* yeah!" All the men followed suit. No one protested when Mick ordered another round of shots.

Fritch liked to blend different flavors in his mouth, then wash them down before the next combination. You could really experiment at a buffet. Now Denny poured for him. All this caring for each other's buzz. Well,...family. The table chatter in the bar washed around them. Silverware and china and glassware chimed like a hundred slot machines. Then the band climbed the stage. They launched into a cover of the Stone's *Let's Spend the Night Together.* A saxophone and two chick backup singers on the side! Pretty classy for *up north!*

Fritch knew he was getting hammered as he swerved toward the buffet a third time. He secured six more shrimp, and another dollop of the mac 'n' cheese to which he added a ladle of au juice from the beef cart. He wasn't concerned when this fluid found its way into the cocktail sauce.

When he was situated for eating again, the band shifted gears into Merle Haggard's "*Fightin' Side of Me.*" He heard the first 'eee-hawws' of the evening. At this, Stan laid down his fork, turning full attention toward the little stage. Suppose they had to cover *those* bases, too, Fritch thought. But the word *eclectic* did not occur to him as it might if he was sober.

"Hey, *dude*! Where's your shells?" Mick called, getting up for his third plate.

Fritch laid another tail on a used plate that hadn't been bussed yet. "Right there! I'm getting a pile of 'em!"

Mick shook his head and laughed. "No, no, man! Those are just the tails! You have to peel 'em." He pointed at the translucent husks on his own plate.

Now Denny and Patrick were roaring. "I didn't notice, dude, and I've been *watching* you scarf those down!" Denny pounded the table.

"What's in there, extra nutrients or something?!" Patrick yelled.

Next to Patrick, Carrie was near tears. "You *know* it's gotta be a vitamin or something," she gasped.

Fritch stared at his remaining food. "Well, geez. What'm I supposed to do now? I eat *bar* shrimp all the time."

"Well, did they ever *crunch* like that?" Denny asked. "Geez. Didn't you see the little fuckin' legs?"

"No! I thought these were just really cold."

Patrick reached to take one of his shrimp. He dipped it and held it toward Fritch's mouth. "Don't worry *now*, bro! Your system is just gonna do what it's gotta do!"

Reaching over Fritch's shoulder, Mick topped off his glass yet again. "Better keep 'em irrigated," he laughed. "And maybe lots of that banana pudding they've got. Smooth everything along."

Fritch continued to crunch. It was probably too late, like they said. Too late to learn how and then futz with the damned things. He spooned on extra sauce. Still not thinking the implications through, he reached for the *Tabasco* in front of Denny and added *that*. Banana pudding, eh? Yes, and he'd seen peach cobbler, too, Terri bringing a great flat pan of it, orange and steaming, from the kitchen.

The band erupted into some of the new power pop or punk or whatever it was: *"What I like about you; you hold me tight; tell me I'm the only one, wanta come over tonight…yeah!"* He'd been clinging to Classic Rock throughout the separation. Several of the wives dropped their forks and tugged his cousins up by their elbows. The dance floor filled, everyone bounding up and down. Faces gleamed with boozy exertion. Fritch wanted to bounce and flail his arms, too. And here he was, still cramming his face. So many *women* in the place. All shapes and sizes. How had he not noticed? Being among family all evening, he hadn't thought about how alone he was. Even Patrick was being dragged up. "Move it, baby," Carrie insisted.

"Who *is* this?" Fritch yelled.

Patrick just shrugged as he was led away.

At least he wasn't penned in. For as long as the tune went on, he could easily make it to the desserts. It was probably time. So *what* if he left a couple of shrimp? Who was counting? No need to further abuse his digestive track. Time for a jolt of sugar. Then ask about black coffee--well, *pretty* soon. See who'd volunteer to drive him to Grandma's, then bring him back for his car in the morning. It looked like Carrie hadn't been drinking too hard. That's probably what Patrick was thinking, too. No need to be stupid.

—␣—

It is Wes, already dressed for the day, wanting into the bathroom. He scrambles in and lifts the seat with a bang as Fritch backs into the hall. Patrick waits there in a ratty bathrobe, coffee mug in hand.

"There's a bathroom upstairs, you know."

Patrick blows on the steaming liquid. "Shower's up there. That's *another* line."

Fritch passes through the living room where his mother is working a cross-word puzzle. Carrie has taken over the embroidery.

"Come here, you," his mother growls.

"Yeah?"

She pushes her glasses back up to the bridge of her nose. "Don't you be getting Stan in trouble. Try to set a better example."

"What? *Me?* Where did you get that?"

"I'm just saying." She erases from the newsprint, then scratches her temple with the eraser. "Your Aunt Muriel thinks he might have a problem." She mimes a bottle to her mouth by tipping her thumb.

"Right. OK. I'm on it," Fritch grumbles, moving away quickly.

In the kitchen, his Grandma and his Dad are each stirring scrambled eggs in large skillets. Some progeny of a cousin he can't immediately name slathers butter onto a growing stack of toast. Fritch jumps as two more slices leap from the slots. He smells onion in the pans.

In the window behind the sink, smoke rises between two oak trees. The top of a thick rope metronomes through the branches. A tall urn gurgles next to him on the counter, its red light beckoning. "Can I get some of that?"

His father lifts and folds the eggs. "If you can serve yourself."

"What's going on out there?" Fritch leans over the sink to look.

"Beautiful morning. Gramps is grilling."

On a gas grill that looks like a *Star Wars* battle cruiser, Fritch's grandfather is frying bacon in an iron skillet. Sausage links and patties sizzle on the opposite wing. Flames leap at the falling grease as he choreographs, a spatula in one hand and a long fork in the other. He plays the knobs of the burner settings like an old short-wave radio.

"Guess I'll find a seat, then," Fritch says, when he has filled a mug.

"Won't be long," his father says. "Could be a *crowd*, too."

Fritch navigates the back steps gingerly, pausing to sip and sigh. "Hey there, old timer," he calls.

"*There's* my Number One! None the worse for wear, I see."

"Good. I've got *somebody* fooled."

Two picnic tables are pulled together in the side-yard. Little kids dart about from sandbox to tire swing. Stan Brauskas sits at the end of one bench, facing the garage and a small woods at the back of the property. There is no beer, though the pitchers look familiar. Someone has brought out milk, tomato juice, and orange juice. Such a bounty they are experiencing this weekend. Food and fellowship. Seems like all it takes is to pull some tables together. After that buffet, Fritch doesn't feel like making any more choices. But right now, he'd like to guzzle *all* of them, one after another. A stack of plastic cups has been set out. As he circles to sit across from Stan, he sees the stalk of celery in the kid's drink.

"Wow, is *that*…?" He eases onto the bench after carefully placing the coffee in front of him.

"Hair of the dog, dude."

"Well, you're a better man than I."

Stan grins, or grimaces, Fritch isn't sure which. The kid raises red-lidded eyes and winks. "I don't *have* to be." From a pocket in his cargo pants, Stan produces two airline shooters of vodka and a bottle of *Tabasco*. "What can I make ya?"

Down the road, Fritch hears the approach of the Burdette clan from their cottage. The climbing sun is already diamonds on the bit of East Twin water he can see. Someone is going to be bawling pretty soon if they keep trying to do underdogs with that swing. At least all the shrieking will stop for awhile. The tire twirls whenever the pusher passes under it. You have to time it just right, or…Then he remembers that he is supposed to come up with some kind of a toast for later at the reception. It has to be something he can say in a church basement, but they'll all be expecting something *funny*. Well, it's good to be the oldest--most of the time. Maybe until they want him to set an *example*.

"Just make it a *Screwdriver*," he tells Stan. Anything with more hot sauce in it won't be a good idea.

Photo Finish

G wen is leaving for good this time. It's not just a trial run like last year. We went to see a lawyer last week. Then I helped her move. She borrowed a *Suburban* from a girlfriend and I hired Larry, a high-school kid from down the road. You can coax most of a bedroom suite into the back of a *Suburban*, but I'm keeping the bed. Gwen wants the studio couch and the lamp table. The lamp table matches my headboard, but I didn't protest. I cleared the stack of magazines off the top and put the lamp on a TV tray. I know when I'm getting off easy.

It was a long Saturday of wrestling with furniture. Then we had to put everything in the middle of the living room at her new apartment and throw sheets over it. Her landlord wants to paint the place before she takes possession, and she's waiting on a bed delivery from *Art Van*. So, she has to spend one last weekend with me.

The whole ordeal wasn't nearly as emotional as last time because we figured it was coming. But now I just want to throw another log on the fire and watch the Piston game from Milwaukee. Our son Wes is staying with a school chum to play *Dungeons and Dragons,* so I didn't have to fix dinner--just a sandwich and a quick nap. When Wes is home, I feel compelled to provide a hot meal. Tonight, I had smoked turkey breast on rye with Cajun mustard. Gwen wasn't hungry. I popped the top on a can of non-alcohol beer to wash it down. *That* stuff is a Godsend.

The reception coming down our antenna mast from Detroit is almost perfect. That's not always the case so it could be a good omen. Cable doesn't reach our subdivision yet. There is a half-hour until tip-off, so I snooze on the floor.

Gwen is in the tub, lounging with a historical novel. She'll probably watch the game. The first date we ever went on was to a Piston game when they were still playing at Cobo Hall. We saw them lose to the Lakers in overtime. I thought that was pretty impressive for a first date. We had sideline seats behind the scorer's table. Jerry West was in the twilight of his career but, of course, he got the ball for the game-winning jumper. Gwen had an immediate attraction to Wilt Chamberlain. She has made several attempts to acquire sophisticated, liberal attitudes. Unfortunately, she has accomplished most of them while apart from *me*. She's always teasing me about a woman she supposedly slept with last year.

So, this is how Gwen takes a bath while I snooze through the pre-game hype: She allows a continual trickle of hot water so that the temperature will remain consistent. The edge of the tub is lined with paraphernalia--cigarettes, butane lighter, and an ashtray. There are three vessels of beverage and one of feminine hygiene product. A half-empty mug of coffee is abandoned, no longer hot. Her attention turns to a tall glass half full of *Courvoisier* and cracked ice. There are *Star Wars* characters embossed on the sides of the glass as it glazes with condensation. The glass of water for chasing the liqueur is likewise beaded. The toilet is piled with a fresh towel, under-things and night-wear, so I went out on the deck to pee after my sandwich. The moon had not yet risen.

When she finally hoists herself out of the amniotic water, the Pistons are already behind. An ovation from the Milwaukee crowd wakes me, and I hear the drain emptying. The Pistons have called a time-out to avoid an early rout. Gwen carries the *Courvoisier* and an armload of photo albums into the front room.

"Aren't you going out?" A year ago, these questions, posed by either of us, would have been bitter with sarcasm. But the *sundown syndrome*, that burning need of the freshly single to push themselves socially, is no longer an issue. I'm lying on the floor in grass-stained sweatpants and a spattered shirt I used last fall while staining the deck. I haven't shaved since that morning at the lawyer's office.

"I haven't got anything planned."

Underneath the albums is a plush, burgundy robe and glowing flesh. The robe is tied loosely to reveal some copper-freckled cleavage. What is *this?* Last chance for love? One more horizontal thrash to leave me with a taste of what

I'll be missing? Her reddish-brown hair is bobbed short, the way I begged her to wear it for years. I don't have a clue who might have finally talked her into it.

"Because you don't have to entertain *me*," she says.

"No problem," I sigh. "I'm in for the night."

Meanwhile, the ball is back in play. Isiah Thomas walks it over the time line, trying to slow the pace. The Bucks put on a press because they want to run. They have an instinct for the knock-out punch.

"We ought to divide up these pictures then." She plunks the albums onto the carpet between us. There are eight heavy books. The pages are thick. There are five or six pictures on each page, over Gwen's neatly printed captions. The pictures are held in place by a clear, adhesive leaf. There are many photos of kittens playing and kittens with red eyes in the clothes dryer. I can waive these without dispute.

"I don't see why this is necessary. You can look at them anytime you want." The temporary court order has given us joint custody of Wes which means that Gwen will be visiting often. I'm staying with the house because I can afford it, and Wes is staying with the house so that his life won't be *totally* disrupted. We've worked it all out in detail. I hope Gwen will even want to sleep over when the decree wears off. But the earlier, homemade separation agreement didn't have the impact that the court document is likely to have. Some attitude adjustments will be inevitable.

"I want some of them *with* me," Gwen insists. Her tone is one degree above frigid. "I'm leaving *enough* things behind."

I won't argue with that, not if I want to keep things congenial. As I said, I'm getting off easy. I have the kid most of the time, and I can live in this house until the kid graduates. I get to keep half the furniture, the stereo and half the LPs, half the towels, and half the dishes. *All* of the washer and dryer--like that. Gwen took the silver, the china, a nice set of *Farberware*, and a lamp we were given as a wedding present. It needs polishing, but it goes with her pewter objet d'art. She took the new microwave that has all the bells and whistles. I lift an album from the pile.

"What criteria are we going by?" I hope to be denied any photos in which my many in-laws appear. Well, maybe I'll take a few of my mother-in-law who happened to be a cool lady.

"Nothing special. We each take some of everything. There are double prints of some." She begins peeling up the clear sheets, brushing the pictures onto the carpet with her index finger,

Baby pictures. I'm not going to need too many baby pictures. Perhaps I just don't remember all those tender moments the way Gwen does. I was usually wasted by one means or another. I don't recall much of Wes's infancy except the usual nocturnal disruptions--arguments about who's turn it was to drag ass out of bed and feed or change him. Babies aren't really that cute in the crawling stage, if you ask me--sorting through the cat box if you turn your head for an instant. Or applying supper to their faces like it was clown makeup. I didn't really appreciate him until he could speak in rudimentary sentences and throw a ball, however wildly.

"I'll take a few of these from the first birthday." I pick up two, like cards which have been dealt to me. There are *many* from that event: Wes in a high chair, fascinated by the single candle, though morose at the intrusion of new teeth. He has stopped squalling long enough for cake and ice-cream. There *I* am, *Strobs* in hand, coaxing: *Blow! Put it out, buddy!* "He was a cute little bugger, wasn't he?"

"He was a *pistol* that day." Gwen frowns, confirming my spotty recollection.

There are taped interviews and highlights during half-time, then a wide-angle view of the crowd and the empty court. Scoring stats are superimposed on the screen. These show that the game is nearly out of hand for the Pistons.

Gwen won't care about all these Little League scenes. From the lens of an *Instamatic*, the outfield recedes toward a distant sunset. Wes looks like the other fielders, tiny in their baggy uniforms. Parents were allowed to walk the foul lines for photo opportunities. So, there he is in left, close to the camera, with very blond hair draping out of his cap. I toss her some of them--Wes at the plate and Wes on first base after a walk. They are scattered around her like unnaturally shiny leaves. She is studying scenes from an early Christmas--our scraggly tree from a gas-station lot.

Wes is in front of the tree, ripping into his packages. One of those kittens leaps among the bows and ruined paper. Wes is wearing Santa Claus pajamas and a red nightcap on his head. I guess I don't want to see any of *these* tonight. I get up to stretch, then go into the kitchen for another beer substitute. I have used these pictures in the past, when I needed to cry--to force the inevitable human response that most men try to suppress. When the marriage was beyond rescue and we were just trying to camouflage the rubble, I went through spans of immobilizing depression. A quick look in that album, the tears would flow, and my outlook would brighten immediately. I hope Gwen is done wallowing in that, too.

When I come back from the kitchen, the books are abandoned in the center of the floor and Gwen is gone. She hasn't flinched since our appointment with the lawyer. But maybe these memories were the last straw. I hear the door of the spare bedroom closing upstairs. She closes it gently, not slamming it to turn up the drama. There was a time when she was certain to weep just loud enough, just long enough, to keep an argument going. I became incensed at the manipulation of it, then overwhelmed with compassion the next day, when it was too late.

The Pistons have lost the game but are dragging it out. They want to make the score respectable, I suppose. They use their time-outs to set up each remaining opportunity. Each of these pauses is sufficient for two commercials. Then they press all over the floor. They foul intentionally, but the Bucks are flawless from the free-throw line. Twelve points down with less than two minutes left. The announcer can't understand why the fans are streaming toward the exits. *Anything* can happen in the NBA. "They must be pretty confident their Bucks can hold on…*blah, blah,*" the color analyst reasons. The play-by-play guy makes a crack about traffic snarls around Bradley Center. Then, of course, one of them has to say, *It's never over 'til it's over.*

I choose enough pictures to fill one album. As I'm stacking the loose ones for Gwen, I discover one of my favorite poses. Gwen loved to snap surprise underwear studies. In this one, I look *really* bad. I look like Lazarus if the Lord had maybe showed up a few days later. I'm in my skivvies--long johns, wool socks and a long-sleeve undershirt. I've probably had a few cold ones on the way home from the night shift. It's almost the dawn of Valentine's Day if memory serves. Gwen slept on the couch, waiting to give me a present when I stumbled through the door. I'm sitting on the one central floor register above a basement oil furnace of our *older, starter home,* trying to sink my teeth into a huge submarine sandwich. She spent thirty bucks on cold cuts and gourmet cheeses to put that beauty together.

Gwen had just broken off her first affair. She was laying the contrition on pretty thick. So, there I am--beat, maybe a little drunk, and still feeling pretty threatened. The Lebanon baloney and olive loaf, the Amish Swiss, pepper jack and Muenster, the dewy romaine lettuce are hanging out like an epicure's centerfold. The sandwich loaf is wide with a shiny, basted crust. It had to be sliced down the middle and held together with toothpicks. I don't remember what she wrote in the card, but it was probably something conciliatory.

I'll let *her* have that picture. I'm hardly a saint, but I'm not entirely responsible for this break-up. That first crisis was eight years ago, and just a prevue of coming attractions. *Neither* of us played the marriage straight after that. She ought to be reminded.

When the game is finally over the final stats crab up the screen, followed by the production credits. There is a title for anyone who spliced a cable or drove the bus from the airport. I remember actually meeting Gwen's lover at an office party where she worked. She'd finally earned an Associate's Degree in Accounting so she could quit waiting on tables. The guy was an Assistant Comptroller or something. I think we huddled in a corner with the free booze, chatting about the Lions. There are *no* pictures of that, that I'm aware of. He seemed pleasant enough--for a *suit*. I was ignorant of his role at the time. Now it occurs to me that I wouldn't refuse to shake his hand. The encounter might be similar to these disheveled coaches going up the tunnel behind their players. A mini-cam follows them. There are fans leaning down to wave. A kernel of popcorn falls on the shoulder of Scotty Robertson's sport-coat. *They* shake hands while the Buck's coach consoles him: *"Your guys fought back. They never quit." "Yeah, but your guys wanted it more." "There were some calls that could have gone either way." "We just couldn't get any momentum going."* When what they are *really* thinking about is *a shower, the bus to the airport, the next game.*

Doublewide

Hector Fritch woke up to the roar of someone's lawn mower. The blinds were drawn over a window screen, so there was no breeze. The tiny bedroom needed airing out. Booze and…The young woman snored lightly. *She* was the drinker. Or he probably wouldn't *be* here. Snored and breathed with a deep regularity, like she might be conked out for another few hours. There was just enough room for Fritch to swing his feet to the floor. The bed had crowded a small chest-of-drawers into a closet. That's probably why there was no closet door.

He began rummaging around for his underwear, his socks. She wasn't going to wake up. Wow. He had even taken his socks off. Well, *he* was no longer drinking; classed up his act a little. *Someone* had to be mature. But the woman… she wasn't *that* young. He hoped. Being over thirty himself made them *seem* younger. And she might be *troubled*, too, pounding her drinks like that. On and on about the soon-to-be ex, that bastard. *Marci*, right? He'd better remember that. Marci.

The guy was supposedly out of the picture. Fritch would have liked to get Marci to sign some kind of release. Even though he was *so* lonely, and it had been *so* long. She would have signed it, too. Might not have stood up in court, she was *so* blasted. But apparently in great need, herself. Ex down in Texas looking for work, except he took a girlfriend along and Marci found out. So, revenge sex.

Fritch kicked through their clothes and into the hallway. Bit of turned up carpet nearly tripped him. He closed the flimsy, hollow door over the curled carpet. It kinda jammed, but then latched. He headed toward the light of the family room where he thought he'd left his pants. The kitchenette came first so he detoured, looking for the coffee-maker. In luck, there were just enough of yesterday's cold remains in the beaker. He preferred to figure out her microwave rather than search through the cupboards for filters and fresh. This was the only eye-opener he could *have* now, so he was impatient. A rack of mugs stood right there on the counter.

On the other side of a snack-bar, the family room began. He recognized the lay-out. One of the fun things he used to do with Gwen was to tour mobile home lots and walk through the models, planning. She wasn't pregnant yet. They certainly weren't married yet. Hector had quit college and lucked into a sweet-paying job in an auto plant. Half the couples who married in Celeryville ended up in doublewides. The *mobile homes* sprang up on corner lots carved out of Mom and Dad's farm. There was a new park, too--rolled sod, seedling trees, small metal storage sheds.

Fritch carried the over-cooked dregs of coffee past the dining table. He sat down on the battered faux-leather couch. What appeared to be a decent color TV front-and-center; behind it, a panorama of windows wrapping around the bow of the structure. The view was of the street, their cars in the drive, his cautiously positioned behind hers. Fritch blew and sipped.

It was a big riding mower making that racket, scalping one little lawn after another. In a hurry, the guy wore ear-covers and a uniform. A truck from the landscaping service was parked down the street. Another fellow waved a leaf-blower at clippings on the sidewalk. Fritch looked for a coaster. He had to settle for a magazine, *Soap Opera Digest*. He spotted his trousers draped over the back of a hassock. He got up to pull them on, then pulled the button for the television. Seemed like the park was maintained well enough. Maybe this Marci had cable. The picture winked and began to broaden. Uh-oh. Tube going bad.

Fritch eased into the back of the couch. Well worn. He could feel a spring, though the piece didn't seem to be duct-taped anywhere. Place looked clean, the Hollywood gossip magazines in a neat stack. He brought the coffee to his lips again, the steam rising pleasantly into his tired eyes. A small hand tapped his shoulder and he leaped, spilling. "*Je-sus* H. Christ!"

Most of the lost coffee found his neck and t-shirt. One splash made it to the shag carpet, its stain quickly lost in the pattern.

"Who in the *hell*...?"

It was a little boy who'd jumped back from behind the arm of the couch as Fritch whirled. The kid's mouth fell open at the shock he'd caused. "I had a sleep-over at Zak's next door...Hey, you *swore!*"

Fritch placed a free hand, pitter-pat, over his heart. "OK! *Sorry!* But you scared the liver out of me."

The boy added one more step to the distance between them. The summer scalp- job to his blond head was growing back raggedy. At least his mother hadn't forced a queue on him. "You looked like my Daddy. From behind."

Fritch folded the bottom of his tee up to mop his stinging neck. Would the kid know if Mom had aloe in the medicine cabinet? No, can't send him looking for meds. He bent, and daubed a few drops of coffee from the leather. "Yeah, sorry to disappoint you, there, what's-yer..."

"It's OK. Ain't the first time."

"Marci, uh...your Mom didn't say anything about kids at home."

"There's only me, Cee Jay," the boy said.

"Well, I'm Hector, Cee Jay." Fritch extended his hand but the child was still leary of him.

"Is she still sleeping?"

Hector slowly lowered his hand. "Uhhh, yup. Yup. Far as I *know*. Why? Is she supposed to be up?"

Now the boy inched around to the front of the coffee table, idly scratching his abdomen under his pajama top. He aimed a black, plastic device toward the TV and *Scooby Doo* appeared. "She *always* sleeps in on Saturday."

Fritch reclaimed his coffee and sat down again. "But she *usually* goes to work, right? You're, like, the man-of-the-house then?"

Cee Jay stifled a smirk. He had a few baby teeth missing. Fritch guessed he must be at least eight. Three or four years younger than his own son, Wes. "Mom's a *Molly Maid*. My Nana comes over in the summer

Only a half-cup of coffee had survived the spill. Fritch knew he'd have to make a pot if he was going to stay much longer, long enough to be polite. It looked like the responsible thing to do, now. Might be an encore in it if he was polite *and* responsible. "Does Nana come over on Saturday? Ever?"

Cee Jay wandered into the kitchen. "Sometimes." After a clatter of cupboard doors, he emerged with a box of cereal--a store brand knock-off of

Fruit Loops. Under his arm he carried an unopened bottle of orange soda. "She checks up on us."

Fairly certain that men like himself must be the object of Nana's vigilance, Fritch was relieved that he'd put on the pants. The kid placed his drink at the opposite end of the coffee table from Fritch's mug. He sat down then fit a handful of the pastel rings into his mouth.

"You getting enough sugar this morning?" Fritch teased.

Cee Jay crunched the cereal and twisted the cap off the *Faygo*. "Gramma says I gotta have fruit too."

Fritch shook his head. "And are you going to do that?"

The kid swigged. He dug into the cereal box squeezed between his knees. "The bananas are all brown."

Fritch stood up, draining his coffee. "Listen, do you ever eat, like, a real, traditional breakfast?"

"*What* kind?"

"Like with bacon and eggs and toast? Or oatmeal and toast? Mom ever make you pancakes?"

Cee Jay shrugged. "Nana does sometimes. She dips bread in eggs."

Fritch picked at the corners of his eyes. He *had* to make more coffee soon. "Hey, Cee Jay? Do you like *McDonald's*? Know what they've got there now?"

The boy swallowed more orange soda. He licked at crumbs around his lips. "Happy Meal?"

"Yeah, well…yeah. But now they've got this breakfast sandwich. It's pretty cool. It's got everything in it--egg, bacon, cheese."

"They take me there for a treat. When support comes."

Fritch backed toward the kitchen area. "Ya know what, though. I could *make* you one. But you've gotta lay off that junk for a minute. You've gotta show me where stuff is. You wanta help? That monster on there is just gonna be some mean old guy in a costume. They always figure it out."

"OK." Cee Jay put the soda down and folded the box-top catches of the cereal. "I seen it already. I only know how to make toast, though."

Fritch put his mug next to the coffee-maker. "That's OK. That's the last step. But first, can you find where Mom keeps her coffee and filters?"

"Those paper thingy's? Sometimes she has to use paper towel. Boy, *that* makes her swear!"

Fritch opened the refrigerator. Cee Jay soon slipped in under his arm.

"OK, let's just find the eggs and cheese. We better skip the bacon." The kid dug out a carton of *Extra Large Grade A* and handed it to him. Then came a brick of store-brand American cheese in wax paper. "That tub of margarine, too, Cee Jay. *Here* we go! Can you find me the slicer?"

While Cee Jay rattled around in a drawer of utensils, Fritch took a closer look into the refrigerator. The mayo was crusted yellow around the lip of the jar so he put it back. He eyed a poorly sealed package of baloney with the lunch-meat darkening around one edge. Shrugging, he pulled it out. He spotted a bottle of *Ranch* dressing. That's what *he* always used anyway. He wouldn't even ask. Just like with Wesley. You had to just let them bite into the new thing without worrying about it. Now Wes loved *Ranch* instead of *Miracle Whip*. Or whatever that was Marci had.

She'd left a pan of used grease or oil on the stove. Fritch rinsed most of it into the garbage disposal under some surprisingly hot water. Still looked slick enough. Needed just a little marge, maybe. He turned the switch for a front burner. He opened the coffee maker. Shit! Old grounds. But the trash basket was just under the sink. Pretty soon he had the water running through, that sound still a relief.

He cracked four eggs on the edge of the pan and adjusted the electric burner. Cee Jay worked the slicer through the cheese as if he'd done it before. But how *about* that Marci, having a kid. He wouldn't have guessed. Of course, there was no light to check her out by except some streetlight getting in between the blinds. Everything about her was taut enough and when the preliminaries were exhausted he pushed in against a pleasant resistance. Then a nice squeeze pulled on him. Almost difficult to move, but such a pleasure to move slowly. Well, how *could* he last? It had been such a while. She laughed. It was a laugh of enjoyment, he was pretty sure, not *at* him. She didn't seem to mind one way or the other, but he kept going anyway. Then her sighs turned to those of sleep.

Fritch flipped the eggs. Cee Jay had climbed up on a stool by the toaster, his finger poised on the lever. "Now?"

"Sure. Set it for Medium. See right there in the middle? You guy's've got some baloney, ya know. Pig is pig. You ever hear *that* one? I had to trim some of it but, wanta try it?" The boy abandoned his post and came to look at the meat. "Go ahead. Drop 'em right on *those* two in front," Fritch said, when the kid removed two limp slices. "Careful. Careful." He thought he'd better not let him get stung.

But the margarine wasn't spitting much. Fritch flipped again, so the baloney was underneath. The toast ejected loudly. "OK, buddy. Alls we need now are a couple of plates."

Cee Jay offered up a short stack of paper plates from a shelf in the broom closet. Fritch laid the whole works onto the toast, hoping the egg was hot enough to soften the cheese a bit. He pressed on the top slice of bread.

Cee Jay headed straight back to the couch with his plate. "You comin' too?"

Fritch laid out his own sandwich and admired it. He sipped some of the fresh coffee. It looked like he was going to get to meet Nana. Or, face a hungover and likely remorseful Marci sooner or later. He didn't know what the bachelor code required. Maybe it wasn't a hard-and-fast rule. Now *there* was an apt phrase. But there were *so* many latch-key kids, anymore. Maybe it was a grey area. *Many* resourceful, competent kids, who got themselves off the bus and safely inside, fixed their snacks, got themselves across back-lots in the dewy hours after sleepovers. Besides, he didn't know but what Wes might run into strange guys now and then when he stayed at his mother's apartment. "Sure. Yeah, Cee Jay. Let me just top off my mug. What're we watching now?"

"Shazam. You prob'ly ain't gonna like it. You can find the *Stooges* somewheres if ya want. Dad loves them *Stooges.*"

"You're talking *three* Stooges, right? They've got *them* on cable?"

"Somewheres. Hey, what's *on* here? It's *somethin'* different."

Fritch eyed the cable remote, trying to figure out how it might work. "Cee Jay, the best things in *life* are usually something different."

About the Author

Chris Dungey is a retired auto worker living in Lapeer, Michigan with Sharon, his wife of twenty-eight years. He has been writing short fiction all of his adult life. Through the years, more than thirty-five of his stories have been published in small literary magazines; both in print and online. Besides writing, Chris hikes, bikes, sings in a Presbyterian choir, loves to camp at sports car races during summer, and spends too much time at Starbucks in all seasons. He is a long time member of Flint Area Writers workshop. This is his first published collection.

Made in the USA
Charleston, SC
06 May 2014